OWNED BY THE SEA

L.M. SOMERTON

Owned by the Sea
ISBN # 978-1-78686-354-6
©Copyright L.M. Somerton 2018
Cover Art by Emmy @ studioenp ©Copyright May 2018
Interior text design by Claire Siemaszkiewicz
Pride Publishing

OWNED BY THE SEA

Dedication

To all the brave men and women
who save lives at sea.

Chapter One

Jonty stood on the swaying deck and took a last, longing glance at the shore. His stomach was already heaving and the *Caroline*, named after his mother, had only just left the shelter of the bay. The next three days at sea were going to be torment. He hated the annual family ritual that took him away from his painting, but his father insisted on it and, at twenty-five, Jonty still hadn't found the courage to refuse him. Rex Trelawn, who headed a private bank when he wasn't torturing his son, had given up on Jonty ever being a 'proper' sailor, so Jonty was consigned to the galley with orders to keep the rest of the family fed and watered. He dealt with supplies, stocked the cupboards and made sure the boat was ready for a short sea voyage. He was also responsible for reporting their position to the coastguard at regular intervals, which he managed between visits to the head where his stomach contents insisted on making unwelcome reappearances.

The *Caroline* was a forty-six footer and manageable with a crew of four. She was just big enough that Jonty could avoid his father for some, if not all, of the trip. Rex always took the wheel while Jonty's mother and younger sister, Evie, managed ropes and sails with ease. Evie had a sturdy build and relished the challenges of sailing while Jonty favored his recently deceased grandfather, being slight and less than average height. They were a small family, just the four of them, and Jonty found it impossible to refuse the one outing of the year that brought them all together, much as he wanted to. Three days battling his father's disappointment was not his idea of a fun time.

Jonty slipped below deck to the narrow, claustrophobic galley and began preparations for a light supper. Soup and bread, fruitcake and hot chocolate would suffice—not that he'd be able to eat any of it himself. Just the idea of food made his stomach flip over. The four of them would take breaks and sleep in shifts, sailing out past Land's End and into the Atlantic during the night. It would be something of an endurance test but Jonty could cope with that. He kept strange hours when he painted, sometimes forgetting to sleep.

His father was first to descend into the cabin, brushing a hand through his windswept silver hair. He shed his waterproofs, hanging them on a peg before taking a seat at the table.

"Wind's getting up, Jonathon. Be sure to check the shipping forecast later."

"Yes, sir." Jonty didn't need the reminder, but said nothing. He ladled soup into a bowl then placed it in front of his father.

"Not eating?" The usual note of disapproval colored Rex Trelawn's tone.

"No." Jonty didn't expand. His father knew full well that Jonty got seasick every time he sailed.

"Come and join me."

Jonty held back a sigh. He wasn't feeling up to defending himself yet again.

"Shaw tells me your earnings are exceptional for such a young artist. He wants more work from you."

The sigh escaped. "Shaw has no business discussing my finances with you. He's my agent, not yours."

"I hope you're investing well?" Rex waved a soup spoon at him, ignoring Jonty's objection. "I'll have to put the rent up on Cliff House."

Jonty's family, including his sister who was studying at King's College, resided in London. Jonty chose to live at the family's second home in Cornwall where the pure light was perfect for painting. He needed a place of his own where he could cut another tie to his domineering father but somehow he'd never gotten around to house hunting. He didn't rise to Rex's taunt. Housing discussions were preferable to those that questioned his 'dubious lifestyle choices'. Rex Trelawn had never quite accepted his son's sexual orientation and it was a topic best avoided. When Jonty came out at eighteen, Evie had shrugged, his mother had wept for a while then refreshed her makeup, hugged him then commenced trawling her copious address book for prospective boyfriends. Rex had given him the silent treatment for months until Jonty's first gallery showing had sold out. He'd proved to have some worth, so they'd reached a truce of sorts.

"It's time I found a place of my own," he said. "Property is a good investment these days, isn't it?"

Rex grunted. Checkmate had been reached. Rex wanted his son as a live-in caretaker for Cliff House, a place where he had a hold on him. Rex knew it and so did Jonty. "It's time for the shipping forecast."

Jonty switched on the radio then relaxed into the familiar litany of strange names and wind speeds, paying particular attention to Lundy and Sole.

"It's brisker than I expected," Rex muttered. "Bloody weather changes on the toss of a coin. We could be in for a bumpy ride." He cut himself a slice of fruitcake, grinning.

Jonty's stomach did a jig. He just made it to the head in time.

An unpleasant five minutes later, Jonty returned to the cabin to find Evie swapping places with their father at the table.

"Have you been worshiping the porcelain god again, big brother?"

"The boy has a weak constitution," Rex grumbled, disappearing up the steps to the deck.

"And he could eat roadkill on a rollercoaster without retching," Jonty sniped. "You want soup, sis?"

"Only if you haven't thrown up in it." Despite her words, Evie's smile was sympathetic.

"There's nothing left in my stomach. Besides, you're like Dad. You'll eat anything." Jonty did his duty with the soup then watched as Evie demolished the entire bowl and two sizeable chunks of bread.

"Hungry work out there." She grinned. "Dad been giving you grief again?"

"Same as usual." Jonty shrugged. "He won't change."

"Next year when he proposes this trip, tell him to go take a running jump off the nearest pier."

"So says the favored child."

"I'm straight, gorgeous, I love sport and will provide him with grandchildren. You are not straight, far too pretty for a man, refuse to cut your hair, you hate sport and you have a talent he doesn't, which will no doubt

make you richer than him. Of course he loves me best."
She raised her mug of hot chocolate in a toast.

Jonty couldn't help but laugh. "Love you, sis."

"You too. Now get back to work, galley slave. Mum will be down here next expecting five-star service."

"Okay. You be careful up there. The forecast isn't great."

"Nice and bouncy. Just the way I like it."

Jonty groaned. Sometimes he wondered if he and Evie were actually related or if he'd been swapped at birth. He got a fifteen-minute respite before his mother showed up, dripping wet.

"It's getting a bit brisk out there." She shook out her wet outerwear. "I'm starving."

A violent swell threw Jonty from one side of the galley to the other. He banged his hip but managed to save the pan of soup, slamming the lid on. "In your language, 'a bit brisk' translates as blowing a gale. I hope no one wants hot food later. If this keeps up I won't be able to use the stove."

"You're looking a bit green, sweetheart." His mother took the spot Evie had vacated. She chugged down the soup, dunking bread to mop up every drop. "Mmm, fruitcake too, you're spoiling us! Have you eaten?"

"What do you think?" Jonty put a flask of hot chocolate on the table then wedged himself onto the bench.

"Found a nice boy yet?"

Jonty felt giddy. His mother switched from one topic to another more often than she changed her designer shoes. "I'm too busy and, besides, Cornwall is hardly a hotspot on the gay scene."

"Come up to London, then. There's this club I've heard about called The Underground…and another place called Secrets…"

"Mother! Those are BDSM clubs. Your internet history must be fascinating."

"I just thought... The Underground is in a very nice area. Westminster. Probably full of kinky MPs."

"We are not having this conversation. No. Just no." Jonty hid his face in his hands.

"Interesting that you already know what kind of clubs they are." His mother gave him a sly grin.

"I... Eat your fruitcake."

"If you weren't so green, I'm sure you'd be bright red. I'm your mother, not a nun. You and your sister are evidence that I have had sex at some point."

"I think I'm going to be sick again." Jonty ran for the shelter of the head where he slammed the door, grateful for the escape. "My own mother thinks I need to join the leather scene. Oh God, could this nightmare get any worse?" It wasn't that he'd discounted a possible visit to The Underground, which did appeal to him. It just wasn't a topic he wanted to discuss with his mother of all people. The boat lurched to one side then the floor seemed to drop from beneath his feet. Jonty staggered, trying to get his balance in the confined space. A need for air overwhelmed him. He burst back into the cabin to find himself alone.

The swell had increased so Jonty spent a few frantic minutes stowing everything that wasn't nailed down, gaining more than a few bruises in the process. He used the intercom to get an accurate map reference for their position from his father before reporting into the coastguard who warned him of increasingly heavy seas.

"No shit." Jonty grabbed the edge of the table to steady himself. He relayed the information to his father. "Do you think we should turn back?"

"No, of course not. We can ride it out. It's just a squall."

"I think it's a bit more than that," Jonty argued.

"Get some sleep, Jonathon. I'll wake you in six hours. It will all be over then and we'll be wishing for more wind, not less."

"I… Yes, sir." At sea, the captain's word was law and there was no room for dissension. Although with his father that applied at all times, not only onboard the *Caroline*, so Jonty knew he was fighting a losing battle. He did a quick tidy round then rolled into his bunk in the miniscule sleeping cabin, staying fully clothed. He drifted into an uncomfortable doze, rocking from side to side with the motion of the waves, his dreams filled with shipwrecks and towering seas.

* * * *

For Jonty, the next twenty-four hours were a nightmare of nausea and conditions straight out of hell. He'd had little sleep when his sister woke him because he was needed on deck. His father still insisted on pushing ahead with the journey even though the waves were topping twenty feet and growing. Even with his safety line firmly attached, Jonty felt vulnerable, but his mother needed rest so he ignored his roiling stomach and followed his sister's orders. When the wind dropped and he finally got a break he was soaked through, despite his waterproofs, and freezing. His hands and face were raw from salt and wind burn.

"Looks like we made it through!" His father sounded triumphant despite having been at the wheel all night. "I'm going to catch forty winks while Evie takes the wheel." He stomped below, not even glancing in Jonty's direction.

"I don't think this is over," Jonty said, watching the wind whip foam from the tips of the waves. The huge swell had subsided and a glimpse of gold peeked between threatening clouds. "We're in the eye of the storm."

"This isn't a hurricane, Jonty." Evie laughed. "Admit it—Dad was right. We rode it out. As soon as Mum gets back on deck, you can go below and cook. I could use something hot."

Jonty shrugged. He wasn't an expert sailor and his empty guts were hardly a good indicator of conditions, but it seemed to him that the weather had changed too quickly. Conditions at sea were often unpredictable, but he was eager to get back on the radio and check the forecast. If his suspicions were unfounded then great, he'd hold up his hands and bow to his father's superior instincts. "I hope you and Dad are right."

"The wind's good. Help me get the mainsail up, Jonty." His mother appeared next to him.

"How come you look so refreshed?" he asked. "I feel like I slept for about five minutes and that was on a possessed trampoline."

"After years of your father's sailing expeditions, I've learned to sleep anywhere." She smiled. "It was good of you to come along, Jonty. I know you'd rather be anywhere else."

Jonty helped with the sails then headed below. He had stashed pre-cooked chili that just needed heating through. His stomach rebelled at the thought of eating anything, but the others would appreciate the hot food. Once the meal was underway, he checked the forecast. The satellite images made for uncomfortable viewing. From what he could tell, the *Caroline* had passed through the edge of one storm and was currently riding a gap between two more. The boat was being funneled toward a potential convergence. It was still possible that the storm centers might dissipate and Jonty prayed that would happen. He got on the long-range radio to contact the coastguard.

"This is the *Caroline*. Repeat, this is the *Caroline*. Any update on prevailing conditions?"

"*Caroline*. Glad to hear from you. We were starting to worry."

"It was a bit hairy for a while but we're through without damage."

"You didn't turn back?"

"No... Please hold while I get current coordinates." Jonty radioed his sister to check their position, then reported back.

"Not good, *Caroline*. You're headed into a real mess out there."

"I see it." Jonty sighed. "Any sign of separation?"

"Met. Office says convergence is most likely. Can you outrun it?"

"Negative." Jonty took a deep breath. "What's your advice?"

"Batten down the hatches and pray, *Caroline*. Keep us updated and Godspeed."

"*Caroline* out." Jonty sighed. He had to wake his father and tell him the bad news. He ventured into the cabin and for a while stood watching his father sleep. Rex looked younger, less severe, in repose. Taking a deep breath, Jonty shook his father awake.

"What...what is it, Jonathon?" Rex scrubbed a hand through his hair.

"Storms are converging. We're running into trouble with no way out. The coastguard expected us to turn around. They have no advice other than to hunker down."

"You're exaggerating."

"Come and see for yourself." Jonty's patience was running thin.

Rex hauled himself out of his bunk. He pulled on a sweater but had otherwise remained dressed while he slept. "Fine. This better not be a false alarm." As Rex stepped through the cabin door, the boat lurched violently to one side. He lost his balance and pitched forward. Jonty, following behind, tried to catch him but missed and fell himself. There was a sickening crack from his arm as he landed, then a moment of blinding pain.

"Shit. Fuck!" He knew the arm was broken. There were no bones sticking out but his wrist was already swelling. He cradled it, taking deep breaths while the pain subsided to a throb. "Dad, are you okay?" Jonty scrambled to his feet as the boat pitched and rolled, the brief respite in the weather clearly over. He made it into the main cabin and found his father face down on the floor. Blood formed a pool around his head.

"Oh God, no." Jonty dropped to his knees. He tried to see where the blood was coming from. His father was out cold, his head at a strange angle. Jonty swallowed his fear. He leaned down, trying to detect any breath from his father's mouth. He felt nothing, nor could he find a pulse. "You can't do this now, you fucker." Jonty's anger overwhelmed him. A life-or-death situation approached and his father, who'd gotten them into this position, had taken the easy way out. Even with his limited first aid training, Jonty understood he shouldn't move his father in case of a back or neck injury, but he had to balance that with a need to get him breathing. He rolled him over, pushing back his panic as he noted the blood leaking from Rex's left ear. He made sure his father's airway was clear then began mouth to mouth. After what seemed like hours but was no more than a minute, his father gave a small moan. He didn't regain consciousness and his breath was shallow, but he was alive. He was a big man and there was no way Jonty could move him on his own. He shoved a cushion under his head then covered him with an unzipped sleeping bag from the cabin. With Rex as comfortable as Jonty could make him, Jonty got on the radio to his sister.

"Evie, check the satellite — we have big problems and Dad's had a fall down here. He's unconscious." He didn't mention that Rex had stopped breathing for a while, nor that he suspected his injuries to be severe.

"Is he…?"

"He's in a bad way, Evie. Head injury and I've broken my arm."

"I can't leave the wheel, Jonty. Let me tell Mum what's going on. You'd better get kitted up. We're going to need you up here, even with one arm out of action."

Jonty strapped his wrist into a temporary splint from the first aid kit then swallowed some painkillers. He did a cursory clean-up of the chili pan, which had crashed to the floor, splattering the spicy meat everywhere. It was a few minutes he didn't have but he didn't want to leave a hazard for someone else to slip on. He struggled into his still-wet gear, shuddering at the cold before making his way onto the deck and into hell. It was hard to tell whether it was day or night. The angry purple and black clouds merged with the sea. The noise assaulted Jonty's ears, with the howl of the wind challenging the roar of towering surf like two predators fighting for dominance. Jonty got his safety line attached then worked his way forward. He could just make out his mother through the spray. When he reached her, she grabbed his shoulder, holding him close.

"We need to show as little sail as possible. Get the main down and the storm jib up. Once we've done that we'll assess our position." She had to scream to make herself heard. She didn't ask about Rex, but Jonty could see the fear in her eyes. "Your arm. Can you do it?"

He nodded — it wasn't as if he had a choice — then set to work. The stinging spray blinded him and only his gloves prevented the skin from being flayed from his hands. At one point the ship rolled almost ninety degrees before righting itself. Jonty fell, slithering across the deck before he managed to grab hold of a stanchion and get some purchase. The pain made him sick and he retched. He hauled himself up then lurched toward his mother. "This is crazy. We're fighting a losing battle. We need to send a mayday."

An ear-splitting crack sounded above his head. He glanced up then dived for cover as the mast toppled like a felled pine, bringing the rigging with it. Jonty hit the deck, covering his head with his arms. He sprawled, rolling with the movement of the waves, expecting to be crushed at any moment, but the blow never came. He tried to rise but ropes were tangled around his ankles. Between them and the rolling pitch of the boat it took an age to struggle to his feet.

"Mum!" Frantic, Jonty peered through the spray. A huge wave crashed over the side of the boat, knocking him down again, soaking him, filling his mouth with saltwater. He retched as he struggled to his knees. He gave up attempting to stand and crawled toward the downed mast. His hand made contact with a rubber boot, then a leg. Scrubbing the water from his eyes, Jonty struggled to comprehend what he was seeing. His mother's legs stuck from beneath the mast, which had fallen across her chest. When he climbed over it, he could see she was gone, crushed beneath its weight, her sightless eyes open and staring at the sky. A sluggish stream of blood, diluted by the rain and spray, trickled from her mouth. Jonty screamed his anguish into the wind, the sound torn away in an instant. Intense cold and pain permeated every atom of his being. "Evie." *I have to get to Evie.*

Evie had lashed herself to the wheel but it had been ripped from her hands.

"The steering's gone, Jonty. The rudder must have sheared off. Where's Mum?"

"She's gone." Jonty sobbed his response. "She's dead, Evie. The mast…"

Evie froze, her mouth open in a soundless scream. Jonty pushed aside his own emotions. "Get below. There's nothing you can do up here. I'll send up a flare. You try the radio. The waves are too high to launch the life raft. Our best chance is to stay with the boat." He untied the rope around Evie's waist. "Keep the safety line on until you're through the cabin door." She nodded, though Jonty suspected it was an automatic response. He ripped off his gloves then groped in the locker beneath the wheel for the flare gun. Working with one good but frozen hand meant getting it loaded took an age and, when he finally fired the arc of light into the sky, Jonty had little hope it would be seen. The flare lit the deck and, to Jonty's horror, he saw Evie attempting to reach their mother.

"Evie! No!" Jonty scrambled after her, half crawling as the deck dropped from beneath his feet. He grabbed her. "There's nothing you can do. Get below!"

"We can't leave her out here, Jonty."

"We can't shift the mast, Evie. What are you hoping to achieve apart from killing yourself?" Jonty knew his words were hard but they were necessary. He hauled his sister back toward the cabin door then half shoved her through, releasing her lifeline at the last minute. She staggered down the steps where she collapsed in a heap on the floor. Jonty fought the door until it closed before falling next to her. He groaned as his broken arm was jarred.

"See how Dad is, Evie," Jonty snapped. He dragged himself to the radio. "Mayday, mayday, this is the *Caroline*. Our mast is down and rudder gone. We have casualties needing urgent assistance. Mayday. Mayday." The handset was ripped from his grasp as the boat tilted and this time kept going. Pots, pans and crockery became a barrage of missiles as the boat turned turtle and, for a few seconds, Jonty found himself on the ceiling of the cabin. The boat righted itself and Jonty slithered down a wall, crashed into a cupboard and finally came to rest beneath the table. Water sloshed around him, the level above his knees. A warm trickle ran down his cheek and he brushed at the sensation, his hand coming away stained with blood.

"Jonty?" Evie crawled toward him, her skin bone-white. "I think I broke a rib."

"I'm here." He wedged himself into a corner then pulled Evie against him, being as gentle as he could, putting her back to his chest.

"Dad's… He's…gone."

"Hush." He smoothed his sister's dripping hair, not wanting to accept the implications of her words. "It's going to be okay."

"I don't want to die, Jonty."

"We'll be fine. I'm sure help is on its way," Jonty lied. He was so tired. His vision blurred and tears rolled down his cheeks as grief swamped him. Evie stilled in his arms and he couldn't decide whether it was a good or bad thing. She was exhausted, probably hypothermic and in shock, but he couldn't wake her. Her breath came in slow rasps. He had never felt so alone. He closed his eyes and let the darkness take him.

* * * *

"Remind me again why we do this?" Jed Curnow peered into the gloom and rode the rise and fall of the lifeboat as it cut a path through mountainous seas.

"It's our fetish for getting cold and wet." Kennick Poldean, coxswain of the boat and currently manning the wheel, grinned. "That and the whole not getting paid for risking our lives thing."

Jed grunted. "Of course it is. Why didn't they send the Newquay boat out on this one?"

"Already on a shout, along with every other boat on the north Cornwall coast and the Lizard peninsula. It's one hell of a night. Some yacht race off southern Ireland is tying up the Irish boats and the conditions are too dangerous for the flyboys to take off. We're on our own on this one."

"Well, that's great." Jed held on to a rail as the boat plunged from a watery cliff. "So what have we got?" He'd been last to the boat and hadn't picked up the details before it had rolled down the slipway. The first hour at sea had been about navigation, ensuring everyone knew what they were doing and overseeing operations while Kennick focused on driving the boat through the waves.

"A yacht, the *Caroline*, out of Newquay. Family of four on board. All adults. We don't know much other than their last reported position. Their final mayday stated they'd lost the mast and steering and that they had casualties. The current will be drawing them back toward us, so I reckon we'll reach them in around seven hours."

"One hell of a long time to wait for help." Jed didn't have to say out loud what they were both thinking. The sea conditions were some of the worst they'd ever seen. They'd be lucky to find much left of the *Caroline*.

"Harbormaster says she's well-kept and sturdy. The family are amateur sailors but have plenty of experience. The son had been radioing the coastguard with regular position reports. They were astounded that the skipper didn't turn back when he had the chance."

"Probably thought he could ride it out," Jed murmured, shaking his head. So many shouts they responded to could have been avoided if only people didn't have pride...or egos. It wasn't their place to judge, just to save lives. "I'll get Sara up here to help you, then organize some food and a sleep rota. If we have five hours to go, I don't want everyone falling down exhausted when we get to the *Caroline*."

"Good." Ken's face was etched with lines of concentration. "I'll give Sara a turn at the wheel in a while, before I get an arm wrenched from a socket. Make sure Rory keeps an eye on the engine bay. Last thing we need in this mess is to lose power."

Jed made his way from the wheel house to the main cabin where he checked on the rest of the seven-man, two-woman crew. The waiting was the worst part of any mission for Jed and for most of the others. He made sure people rested as they could, ran through some training drills on paper and doled out food. As deputy coxswain it was his job to ensure Kennick had nothing to worry about apart from getting them to their destination.

Five hours later and even the most seasoned crew members were green around the edges. Jed had eaten, thrown up then eaten again. His stomach had settled eventually but it was difficult in the rolling seas. There was little rhythm to the huge waves and moving around was dangerous in itself. He ventured back to the lifeboat's small bridge.

"We're nearing the last known position," Kennick said. "All eyes on lookout, Jed. Safety lines double-checked please."

"Dawn's breaking. We'll have some light at least." Jed donned his own gear—as a designated swimmer his waterproofs and lifejacket went on over a dry suit—and took one of the forward positions. Dawn meant little more than blackness turning to dark gray. The howl of the wind and crashing waves were deafening. Jed could taste nothing but salt and he held tight to the guardrail, grateful for the deep cleats on his boots that gave him grip. He gave a thumbs-up to those of his colleagues he could see, then fixed his eyes on the water, trying to pick out anything out of the ordinary as the boat's searchlights swept the waves. For an hour or more, the lifeboat combed the seas and Jed was on the point of giving up. They hadn't spotted anything, not even the smallest speck of debris. Then, through the gloom, an arc of light split the heavens.

"Flare!" The cry went up from several people. Kennick turned the boat in the direction of the distress signal. Jed moved further forward and within minutes caught sight of the *Caroline* as it crested a huge wave before crashing in an uncontrolled drop into the trough. Jed headed into the bridge.

"Someone's alive over there," Kennick commented. "Flares don't fire themselves."

"True. It's going to be a bastard to get alongside."

"Yep."

Sara, standing next to Kennick, was on the long-range radio reporting the find.

"That's good news, *Govenek*. Keep us informed. You should get a break in the weather in half an hour or so. Wind's dropping to force four to five."

"Thanks, Coastguard. *Govenek* out." Sara replaced the receiver.

"I want you out on deck now, Sara. This is going to be dicey," Jed ordered.

"Sure. Just give me a couple of minutes to suit up."

"She's a good lass," Kennick said.

Jed nodded. "That she is. Reckon we'll need to get a line over to the *Caroline*."

"I'll leave that with you, Jed."

Jed was about to head back outside when the door burst open, letting in a blast of cold air. Rory leaned in.

"Body in the water!"

"Time to go fishing." Jed followed his crewmate outside.

"He, or she, just kind of rolled overboard, Jed. Didn't jump. He's wearing a life vest but…"

"Okay. I'm going in." Jed wriggled into the harness attached to a lifeline. It was rare for him to get in the water in such bad conditions, but in this case it was a life-or-death situation. "Get ready to fish us out of the drink." Giving a thumbs-up in the direction of the bridge, Jed clambered over the side and threw himself away from the boat. He caught glimpses of yellow and orange as the stricken sailor bobbed in the water. Waves crashed over Jed's head as he took the few short strokes needed to reach the victim, who wasn't conscious. He grabbed him under the arms and the safety line pulled taut as his crewmates hauled him and his burden back to the lifeboat where they were both heaved over the side. Jed sat against the rail, gasping, grateful for his dry suit but still experiencing the intense cold to his hands and face. The rest of the crew dealt with the casualty, getting him below where he'd be wrapped in thermal blankets. Jed had only caught a glimpse of an ethereal beauty with sodden white-blond hair. He didn't know whether he'd rescued a man or a woman.

Once he'd recovered his breath, Jed supervised the firing of a tow line onto the *Caroline*. They would have to wait for the huge seas to subside before they could begin towing or get a man on board the other boat to search for survivors. It was going to be a long day.

* * * *

When the *Govenek* finally chugged back into harbor nearly twelve hours later, the crew was exhausted. The rescued sailor hadn't regained consciousness, though Jed now knew him to be Jonathon Trelawn, son of the *Caroline's* owner. He'd witnessed the slight figure, swaddled in heated blankets, being cared for by the crew's medic but had been too busy for any closer examination. Once the weather calmed a bit, two of the lifeboat crew took the small dinghy across to the *Caroline* where they reported the discovery of three bodies. One on deck and two below. The somber atmosphere on board the *Govenek* reflected the tragedy.

Friends and family were waiting at the lifeboat station when the crew wearily dragged themselves inside. Volunteers who hadn't been on the shout would deal with the aftermath of the rescue and put the boat to bed. Kelly Miller, a friend of Jed's who owned a beach café, was waiting with Jed's enormous Newfoundland, Marmite.

"Bad business, Jed," Kelly said, his expression serious.

Jed dropped to one knee to give Marmite a hug. The dog treated him to a good licking, then rolled on his back to have his belly rubbed. "One live one's better than none," Jed grunted.

"True. Get yourself home to bed. You need me to come with you?"

"No. Thanks for taking care of Marm, Kelly. I appreciate it."

"Hey — anytime. He's better company than you." Marmite confirmed the statement with a deep bark.

"Cheeky sod. I'll be in tonight for dinner. Save me something edible." Jed gave his mate a wave before heading along the quay toward home. He needed a hot shower to rid his hair and skin of salt, then sleep. Lots of sleep. And just for once, he might allow Marmite to join him on the bed. He needed cuddles too.

Chapter Two

Ten months later

The view of the bay reflected Jonty's mood — unsettled and gray. He stared at the storm clouds gathering on the horizon. The rolling mass of purple, slate and bruise-yellow promised driving rain that would conceal the vista beneath a watery film. The wind was already gusting, whipping the tops of the waves into foaming curls. The huge bay window, one of the few things Jonty liked about his house, rattled in its wooden frame. It was a good day to paint.

Jonty shifted his easel a few inches to the left. He rolled his shoulders. Anyone watching might have assumed he was readying himself for some sporting event that required loose muscles and a focused mind. He squeezed some new daubs of paint onto his color-stained palette, selected a wide, bristled brush and glared at the blank canvas in front of him. Thunder rolled from one side of the bay to the other — Jonty felt the vibrations through the soles of his bare feet. He narrowed his eyes, absorbing the ever-changing light show before him. A few flicks of his wrist mixed the color he needed then he attacked the canvas with his brush as if the white oblong was a personal insult.

Hours later—Jonty had no idea how long—his arm hung at his side, hand clutching a brush so tight his fingers cramped. He threw it onto the palette before clenching and stretching his abused fingers. The finished work was a mesmerizing reflection of wild weather, the colors merged and blended in a way that made them seem alive. Jonty knew it was good but the knowledge gave him little pleasure. He retrieved his phone from his back pocket, took a snap of the picture then emailed it without a subject line or comment to his agent. He counted backward from thirty. At five his mobile vibrated. He waited a few moments before answering—he didn't enjoy talking to people, whether in person or remotely.

"Trelawn."

"Jonty, you fucking genius. Have I told you recently how much I love you? How long before this is dry? I could be convinced to switch teams to get my hands on it."

Jonty held back a sigh. "And this is why I live in Cornwall, as far away from you as possible, Shaw." Shaw Carney was so far from Jonty's type that even if he hadn't been as straight as an arrow, Jonty wouldn't have ventured within ten meters of him. He was a great agent, though, and an honest one. In the cutthroat art world, that made him worth putting up with.

"Don't be like that, Jonty. You know I have your best interests at heart. I can sell anything you paint, you know that. I have a waiting list of buyers chewing on my flesh like starving zombies just for the chance to bid on your work. You have to throw me a crumb every now and again if only to keep the ravaging hordes at bay. Show some humanity."

"Could you be any more dramatic?"

"Oh, there's plenty more where that came from. Tell me I can have it."

"You can have it." Jonty pictured Shaw's expression, happy as a golden retriever who'd been thrown a bone when behind the amiable façade sat a Rottweiler ready to chow down on some unsuspecting buyer. "On one condition."

"Which is?"

"I'm going to ask for your support for something I'm planning. I can't give you details yet but I can promise it won't cost you anything."

"Nothing dangerous, illegal or potentially harmful to my health?" Shaw sounded suspicious.

"No more than that bottle of vintage port I know you glug down every weekend." Jonty switched the phone to his other ear. He knew Shaw would agree to pretty much anything to get his hands on the painting, which would fund his addiction to very expensive wines for the next decade.

"Deal." Shaw chuckled. "I hope I haven't just been out-maneuvered. What the heck. I like you, Jonty. What can I expect from you next?"

Jonty had known the question would be asked—it didn't make him any more prepared to answer it. "If the moment comes, it comes." He never knew when the urge to paint would come over him. Before the accident, it had been all he wanted to do. Now he had to wait for a break in the sterile emotions that clouded his creativity, which usually meant an extreme of depression or a temporary high. Most of the time he simply existed, but it had been almost a year. He wanted to live again, to paint for the sheer joy of it — and he had an idea for something that might make all the difference. If he could find the courage. "Bye, Shaw." He disconnected before Shaw could say anything else or ask more awkward questions.

For the first time since he started the painting, Jonty took in his surroundings. The floorboards around his easel were paint-stained and littered with discarded rags and empty paint tubes. The air stank of thinners. Jonty's clothes and skin were daubed with a rainbow of sticky color which, because it was oil-based, would not come off easily. His stomach growled and he realized that he hadn't eaten or drunk anything for almost ten hours. He knew without looking that the fridge and cupboards in the kitchen were bare of supplies because he hadn't ordered groceries for a while. It was seven o'clock in the evening in the off-season but he knew of one place that stayed open late. Jonty grabbed an ancient pair of deck shoes to slip onto his bare feet. He had some cash in his wallet so, armed with that and his keys, he ventured into the early evening.

Polruthan had been spared the ravages of the tourist trade because its steep, narrow lanes couldn't accommodate many cars. Apart from access to businesses, vehicles other than those belonging to residents were banned. Even some locals who owned cars kept them in a farmer's yard at the top of the cliff. There was no charge, but most people compensated Simon Argawl, the farmer, with home-grown produce, homebrew of varying strength or an occasional basket of fish, fresh from the ocean. He never asked but accepted the offerings with good grace. Jonty's house was one of those with good vehicular access as it was at the top edge of the village, but he didn't keep a car. He had an aging moped that he never used and his feet. If he wanted to get further afield, he called a taxi or begged a lift. Locals were always open to passengers in exchange for gossip. Jonty didn't have much of that to offer and was too shy to talk much at all, but he had novelty value. The 'reclusive young artist from Cliff House' had been adopted by the good folk of Polruthan, and if some of them had his single status in the back of their minds, Jonty didn't much care. He wasn't interested in their daughters, sisters or female cousins. If they caught on that he was gay, it wasn't mentioned, but he got the feeling that potential boyfriends would soon be lined up if there were any on offer. For a small community, Polruthan was liberal. Its population consisted of artists, surfers, fishermen and farmers. Incomers were welcomed if they didn't abandon ship once the summer season was over and, as far as Jonty knew, there were only a couple of holiday homes in the village. It was a rare thing – a community where people cared about each other and valued their surroundings. Unfortunately for Jonty, the place also held a lot of dark memories.

He ambled through winding back lanes heading continuously downhill until he emerged on the quay. He bore right, following the curve of the bay. At its furthest point, set a little back from the pebble beach, stood a wooden shack. Painted blue, it had faded under the onslaught of wind and rain. A hand-painted sign read *Kelly's Place*. Drawn like a moth to a flame, Jonty headed toward the sounds of chatter and music. When he slipped around the door, warmth and the smell of hot chocolate embraced him like a hug. He couldn't help but smile as he made his way through tightly packed tables to the Formica counter.

"Hey, Jonty. How's it hanging?" The man behind the counter had a tanned, weather-beaten face, blond dreadlocks, bushy beard and smiling eyes.

"Hey, Kelly. Good thanks. Need you to feed me, though."

"You been painting and forgotten to eat again?" Kelly frowned.

"Uh-huh."

"Take a seat. I'll bring it over in a few."

Jonty didn't ask what *it* was. Kelly could always be relied upon to come up with something tasty. He made his way to a corner table, nodding to a couple of people he recognized. Most of the customers were cradling mugs or enjoying Kelly's signature toasted sandwiches. Jonty sank into his chair and closed his eyes. No one would bother him here.

He must have drifted into a doze because the next thing he knew, Kelly was shaking him by the shoulder and putting a plate of mixed bean casserole down in front of him, along with a big chunk of crusty bread and a spoon.

"Eat up. Can't have any of my customers looking starved—I'd lose business."

"Thanks, Kelly. You got a second?"

"Sure thing." Kelly wiped his hands on his apron then pulled up a chair. "People can serve themselves if they're that desperate they can't wait a few minutes."

Jonty spooned casserole into his mouth. Flavors burst over his tongue in a warm, spicy explosion. "Mmm, 's good!" He pacified his stomach with a few more mouthfuls before speaking. "I'm thinking of doing a fundraising event for the lifeboat station—an art auction. You think people would be interested in helping out?"

Kelly's eyes crinkled at the edges. "It's been nearly a year, hasn't it?"

Jonty nodded. "I want to do something. Say thank you. I've waited too long."

"You lost your entire family, Jonty. But if you're ready then I'm sure everyone will help."

"I'll need contributions of art to be auctioned, people to help with publicity, space to hold it, refreshments…" Jonty ate some more of his meal.

"Count me in for help with refreshments," Kelly said. "And I'm sure the local WI will muck in. The landlord at the Crusty Crab is a mate. I can talk to him about a keg or two—or discounted pints." He banged on the table. "Hey, everyone—Jonty's gonna do an art auction fundraiser for the lifeboat. Who's in?"

There was a general yell of support.

Tears prickled in Jonty's eyes.

"You can use this place to coordinate, have meetings, that kind of thing," Kelly offered. "When were you thinking?"

"The last week in April. Not the exact date of the anniversary—the closest weekend, maybe, so more people can make it."

"Have you spoken to anyone at the lifeboat station yet?"

Jonty shoveled down more food before answering. "No. I was going to ask if you knew anyone. I didn't want to just wander in there."

"What you mean is, you're too shy."

Jonty blinked. "Maybe."

"Well, you could be in luck, because Jed Curnow will likely be in before long—he comes in most nights for hot chocolate and a natter or to eat. He's the deputy coxswain on the crew. You can run the idea past him." Kelly glanced at the counter where a queue was forming. "Better get back to it. You'll know Jed when he comes in—you can't miss him—he's six feet six."

Jonty focused his attention on the remains of his meal. He was scraping the last remnants from his bowl when the door opened, letting in a blast of cold air. There was no doubting that the new arrival was Jed. He had to duck to get through the door. Jonty didn't want to get caught staring so he tried to get a good look from beneath his lashes. Jed was broad-shouldered and narrow-hipped with a thatch of dark brown hair and a strong chin dusted with stubble. His lips curved naturally into a smile and his eyes were dark, though Jonty couldn't tell what color from where he sat. Jed had a commanding presence and, while he waited patiently for Kelly to serve him, he scanned the room. His eyes rested on each individual for a moment then moved on. When his gaze rested on Jonty, it took all Jonty's courage not to hide beneath the table. He stared at a fixed point on the floor, counted to ten and when he raised his head, Jed's attention was elsewhere.

Letting out the breath he hadn't realized he'd been holding, Jonty tried to decide whether to stay or make a run for the exit. Before he could make up his mind, his light was blocked by someone standing in front of his table. He hardly dared look up but he found the courage from somewhere.

Blue. His eyes are blue. Like cornflowers on the cliffs.

"Kelly said you'd like a word." Jed held out a hand. "Mind if I join you?"

Jonty allowed his own hand to be engulfed by Jed's huge paw. The crushing grip Jonty feared didn't happen. Jed's hold was gentle and warm.

"I...yes...no... I mean I don't mind at all, please do." Jonty shuffled his seat to one side to make more room. He couldn't help but notice how Jed's thighs, wrapped snugly in faded denim, only just fit beneath the table. "I'm Jonty."

"The artist from Cliff House. I know." Jed grinned. He put his mug of hot chocolate on the table. It was topped with a pile of whipped cream and chocolate sprinkles. "Every man needs a vice. Kelly's chocolate is mine. He makes it properly—none of that powdered rubbish. He melts chocolate into the milk while it heats." He took a sip and cream clung to his lips. Jonty had a sudden urge to lick them clean and lost the power of speech.

"Kelly said you had an idea about raising some money for the lifeboat. We're always on the scrounge for cash so anything you can do would be great. We should be replacing the boat, but that's way out of reach. Getting some new equipment would make the crew very happy, though, I can tell you."

"Art is what I know. I thought an auction might draw some interest, especially if I got local craftspeople and artists involved."

"I hope you get more paint on your canvases than you get on yourself." Jed gave Jonty's color-splattered clothing a pointed glance.

"Sometimes." Jonty's cheeks heated. He stared at his empty dish.

"Hey, I didn't mean to embarrass you." A finger beneath Jonty's chin pushed his head up and he let himself be guided. "I'm well known for sticking my size fourteens in my mouth."

"Wow, you have big feet!" The words slipped out before Jonty could stop them. "Oh God. Did I just say that?"

"Well you know what they say… Size is all relative." Jed winked. "Look, I've got to go but I'm here around this time most nights. Meet me here tomorrow and we can talk some more."

Jonty got the impression he was expected to comply. All he had to do was nod. He was glad not to have to think about options or make a decision. "Okay."

Jed nodded as if he had expected no other response. He got to his feet, towering over Jonty. "I'll look forward to it." Then he headed for the door.

Jonty followed a few minutes later, feeling a bit shell-shocked. He was probably reading far too much into just a few sentences but he got the sense that Jed might play for his team. He dismissed the idea as wishful thinking. His overactive imagination was playing cruel tricks on him. The walk home in the cold night air would clear his mind and remind him there was nothing wrong with being alone.

Chapter Three

Jed threw open the shutters on his cottage windows shortly after sunrise the next day. He hadn't slept well, so rather than toss and turn in his bed, he'd risen even earlier than usual—much to the delight of Marmite.

"Breakfast first, Marm, then a walk along the quay. We can see what the lads have brought in for our supper, can't we?" The dog responded with a short bark of agreement before sitting in front of his bowl with an expectant expression. Jed filled it with a mixture of wet food and biscuits, then gave Marmite the command to eat. The food disappeared in seconds.

"It's no good you giving me that mournful look," Jed said, refreshing the dog's water dish. "You always eat too fast then wonder where it all went. The food's in your stomach, you daft dog." He watched as Marmite drank, sloshing water over the flagstone floor as he did. "I swear you get more water on the floor than in you." Jed mopped up the mess with a cloth. "My turn now." He set a frying pan on the hob, lit the gas burner beneath it then added a splash of oil. "And I feel the need for bacon." Marmite tore round the kitchen, barking with excitement. Jed let him have his way for a minute or two then issued the command, "Sit! Or you've less chance of a rasher than catching that ginger moggy from Baker's Lane." Marmite sat, tongue lolling from his mouth, doggy grin fixed on his face. "At least you obey orders. I wonder if the youngster I met last night will be so inclined. I think we might have to find out, don't you?" Marmite woofed his agreement.

Jed hummed as he cooked. It was a crisp, cold morning—just the kind he enjoyed. His kitchen was filled with the scent of frying bacon and there was a new challenge on the horizon. The local gay community was so small Jed often wondered if he might not be part of an endangered species—one that would definitely benefit from a reintroduction program. If they could do it with wolves in Scotland, why not gay guys in rural Cornwall? Having been presented with the perfect excuse to get to know Jonty Trelawn was akin to winning the lottery.

Constructing the perfect bacon sandwich was an art. Thick slices of crusty white bread from Annie Porcowski's bakery, organic butter from Simon Argawl's farm shop—which was where the bacon also hailed from—and just a dab of tomato ketchup. Jed sawed the enormous doorstop in two then took a seat at the table. He admired his work for a second before taking a bite.

"Oh my God, that's good," he mumbled around his mouthful. Marmite whined. Jed took pity and gave him a spare rasher, which disappeared quicker than he could blink. Apparently satisfied, Marmite ambled to his bed, picked up his favorite soft toy—a partly chewed plush lobster — then settled in for a nap. "Don't think you're getting out of that walk, lazy hound." Marmite opened an eye at the word 'walk', but didn't budge. Jed shook his head. "Candidate for most bone-idle animal on the face of the planet." He got back to devouring his sandwich and let an image of Jonty Trelawn fill his mind. *Damn but that man's pretty.* Jed's dick twitched. He had no problem imagining what Jonty might look like beneath his paint-splattered clothes, and could easily picture him naked, bent over a convenient flat surface with his hands tightly bound at the small of his back while Jed…

"Hellfire. Time for that walk." Jed shoved his chair back from the table. He rinsed his crockery, leaving the plate and mug on the draining board to dry. "Come on, Marmite, let's you and I get some exercise." He shoved Marmite's lead in his pocket just on the off chance that something tempted the dog to stray. He left the cottage via the back door, not bothering to lock it. Marmite ambled at his heels while he traversed the narrow back lane behind the house but as they emerged onto the street, Marmite picked up his pace and set off toward the quay like a dog on a mission. Jed's cottage had once belonged to a fisherman, just as many of the properties closest to the shore had. His had the advantage of a spacious shed attached to it — once used for repairing nets and gutting fish, it now housed his bespoke carpentry business. It sat less than thirty feet from the water at the center of the curving bay. The walk to the far end covered roughly half a mile, partly on the sea wall and partly along the shingle and pebble beach. Marmite loved the water and was a strong swimmer — he didn't seem to notice how dick-shrinkingly cold it was. At this time of year, Jed only had to look at the waves and his balls tried to retreat inside his body.

Jed set off at a brisk pace, skirting lobster pots stacked in haphazard piles. All that remained of the village's once extensive fishing fleet—two small trawlers—bobbed at anchor having returned from a night's work. Three men were sorting boxes of iced fish and a van, used to distribute the catch to local restaurants and fishmongers, stood ready.

"What do you have for my supper, boys?" Jed called. Marmite gamboled across and got lots of ear scratches for his trouble.

"Plenty of good herring, Jed. Some nice monkfish. Can't offer you crab—they're all reserved for the St. Croix."

Never having eaten at the five-star hotel, Jed could only imagine what they would create with the crabs. "I'll take some monkfish tail." He loved the meaty fish simply grilled with a little garlic butter.

"You'll pick it up on your way back?"

"Will do." Jed's routine was well known. By the time he and Marmite got back, the fishermen would be heading home to their beds. If they were gone, they'd leave his fish on the quayside and he'd find them later in the Crusty Crab to settle up. Marmite, with the force of a small Sherman tank, head-butted his thigh. "All right, all right! Supper is sorted. We can go, bossy dog." Marmite set off at a jog and Jed followed at a much more sedate pace, tracing the line of the cove. He took the steps down onto the beach and crunched his way along, taking in the shore's symphony. The crash of waves breaking was followed by the maraca shake of shingle sliding back to the water. Gulls wheeled and called above his head and the wind whistled around the headland. The air tasted of salt and was scented with seaweed exposed by the receding tide. Marmite paddled in the shallows but didn't seem to fancy a swim. He poked his nose into rock pools, disturbing small crabs and marooned fish. Jed spotted a starfish clinging to the underside of a limpet-coated rock. He picked up a piece of driftwood then lobbed it in a high arc. Marmite pelted down the beach, kicking up the shingle. He retrieved the wood then returned with it in his mouth, expression full of pride.

"Clever dog!" Jed repeated the throw and retrieve process at least a dozen times before Marmite got tired of the game. The mutt was easily pleased. His daily walks with Marmite gave Jed valuable thinking time, especially when the weather was good and he wasn't more concerned with avoiding hypothermia. He reached the point on the beach where he could see the whole village, clinging to the sides of the valley in a jumble of pastel-colored blocks. There was a scattering of thatched rooves amid warm, terracotta tile and dark gray slates. The oldest cottages, like Jed's, were closest to the sea. Above them, Victorian and Georgian properties jostled for space, their chimneys pointing skyward. Jed could just make out the whitewashed frontage of Cliff House, where Jonty lived. He wondered if Jonty was looking out of his window, trying to make out the figure on the beach. It was fanciful but Jed waved just in case.

Almost a year ago, Jed had pulled a man, half-drowned, from the sea near a sinking yacht. That man was Jonty. It had been a horrific night, which had cost several lives. Jonty's rescue had been the one bright spot in an otherwise dark experience. In all his years on the lifeboat, Jed couldn't remember an angrier sea.

Even amidst the fight to save lives, Jed had noticed Jonty's almost ethereal beauty but, though he knew Jonty had stayed in the village, he hadn't felt able to approach him. He didn't want to be a reminder of that awful night, but now it seemed that Jonty had decided to live again. Jed hoped that if he trod carefully he might stand a chance of getting to know the young man better. Jonty hadn't seemed to recognize him the previous night in the café but that didn't surprise Jed. He'd be amazed if Jonty remembered much at all from the rescue — he'd been fighting for survival after all — and had hidden away ever since.

Jed picked up a couple of smooth, flat pebbles. He walked down to the tideline, Marmite bouncing around him. He skimmed the first stone, which promptly sank. "If this one bounces more than six times, Marmite, I'm taking it as a sign that Jonty Trelawn will be mine." He stood sideways, legs braced and knees slightly bent. His wrist action was perfect. The stone skipped over the surface of the water and Jed counted five, six, seven bounces before it sank. He grinned and ruffled Marmite's fur. "It's going to be a fine day, Marm. I can feel it." On the way home, Jed stretched his legs and picked up the pace. Marmite covered twice the distance he did, charging back and forth, chasing then running from the waves. The breeze was onshore, throwing spray into Jed's face. He ran a hand through his damp hair, glad that it was short. Jonty's long blond tresses would be a tangled mess by now. *He really got into my head, didn't he?* Jed's smile was wry. He almost forgot to pick up his fish from the quay but Marmite's nose led him to the paper-wrapped package. The fishermen were gone — there were just a couple of gulls picking scraps of fish guts from the ground. Jed made a mental note to visit the Crusty Crab at lunchtime to settle up.

His cottage didn't have much of a garden, just a walled backyard where he grew a few vegetables in pots. Marmite nosed through the gate. "A quick wash-down for you, Marm, then a shower for me," Jed said as he picked up the hose attached to the outside tap. On colder days he'd wash the salt from Marmite's fur in the shower, but today it was warm enough to use the hose. Marmite thought it was a great game, dashing in circles, chasing the spray. Washing him off didn't take long then Jed waited for the big shake-down. Marmite seemed to quiver from his nose to the tip of his tail as he shook out a shower of water droplets. Then they went inside and Jed left the dog snoozing in his bed in front of the Aga while he went to take a quick shower.

Twenty minutes later he was clean, dressed in his regular work clothes of jeans and a varnish-stained white T-shirt and armed with a Thermos mug of milky coffee with one sugar. He left the door between the cottage and the workshop ajar so that Marmite could get in when he'd finished drying off. The familiar smell of wood, stain and varnish assaulted his nostrils — it always took a few minutes until he stopped noticing it. His workbench was clear, his tools neatly racked. Pieces of furniture in various stages of completion lined one long wall. Jed gave a deep sigh of satisfaction. He liked his world to be orderly and disciplined.

In his head he lined up the jobs for the day. First off he needed to give a final check-over of a bookcase, a bespoke piece for a local businessman, that was being collected around noon. Jed had enjoyed crafting the white oak piece with its clean, smooth lines. Then he had a matched set of blanket boxes to finish with a coat of wax. He needed to put some time in on a side table commissioned by a local National Trust property, which needed to duplicate the original already in its possession, and finally, if time allowed, he had to pay a visit to St. Peters where a couple of the ancient pews needed some running repairs. All in all, it promised to be a satisfying and enjoyable day. Jed loved the variety of his job. No two days were the same and, though he worked alone, there was never time to be lonely. A constant stream of visitors always rocked up at his door throughout the day. He'd lived in the village his whole life—his family had resided there for several generations—and he had a lot of friends.

He checked the bookcase and had covered it with a clean white cloth before Marmite wandered in. After a few ear scratches, he settled in his usual position on an old blanket next to the outside door where he would keep watch over his empire and suck up affection from every passer-by who spotted him. Marmite had even more friends than Jed, which was proved five minutes later when Arnie, the butcher's redheaded, freckled apprentice, dropped by with a marrow bone that could have come from a brontosaurus.

"Hey, Jed."

"Morning, Arnie."

"Okay to give Marmite a bone? Mr. Settick sent me over here with it."

"Sure. Best do it before Marm floods the entire village with drool."

Arnie set the bone in front of Marmite who immediately placed a possessive paw over it and gave a bark of thanks. "Better get back."

"I suppose, when your boss has a personal collection of meat cleavers, it's wise to be punctual."

"Sure is." Arnie grinned. "Oh, and he asked for a quote for a new butcher's block. He wants me to have my own to train on."

"He spoils you almost as much as Marmite," Jed said. "Tell him thanks for the bone and I'll drop by tomorrow with the quote."

Arnie departed, leaving Jed to wonder about how a steady job and a firm guiding hand had turned a young tearaway into a conscientious and respected member of the village. Jed wouldn't be surprised if Arnie became manager of the butcher's one day. Jed had mulled on the idea of finding himself an apprentice but so far hadn't come across anyone suitable. He'd decided not to force it. The right person would come along one day. He set to waxing the blanket boxes, wondering if Jonty fell into the 'time is right' category. *Perhaps I could take him on as an apprentice sub.* Jed grinned. That idea had a whole range of interesting possibilities.

The morning passed quickly with Jed picking up two new commissions — a fancy mirror frame for a family wanting a special golden wedding gift for their parents and a full set of garden furniture for Sir Michael and Lady Benseddon, regular customers of his. He'd have to start a waiting list soon or he'd have more work than he could cope with, which was a great position to be in. Just before midday the bookcase was collected then he cleaned up a bit before he and Marmite headed to the Crusty Crab for a pint and a spot of lunch, leaving his 'Gone to lunch' sign hanging on the door. Anyone who needed him urgently would know where to look for him.

Marmite knew where he was going so Jed allowed him to take the lead. The Crusty Crab was only one street back from the harbor and still catered to the fishing community it had served since the sixteen hundreds. Jed had to duck low to get through the door to the snug, which was already crowded and noisy. A fire blazed in the enormous hearth that took up one wall and a small cluster of wooden tables and mismatched chairs formed a rough semicircle around it. Jed greeted a few of the regulars on his way to the bar. Marmite wedged himself beneath the vacant table in the bay window.

"Your usual, Jed?" Beth, the barmaid, who had worked at the Crab for as long as Jed could remember, gave him a warm smile.

Jed nodded. "And a round of crab sandwiches, thanks, Beth."

"You take a seat, love. I'll bring it over. Here's Marmite's drink." Beth handed over a metal bowl of water, which Jed laid on the floor near Marmite.

"That dog gets the best service in 'ere." The comment came from Saul Tregarn, a retired fisherman who habitually propped up the bar at lunchtime nursing his half-pint of bitter for as long as possible. Marmite gave a gruff bark then stuck his head in the bowl for a drink.

"That's because he's polite and causes less trouble than the rest of you," Beth replied. "Especially you, Saul Tregarn." She wagged her finger at him and got a wink in return.

"Come and join me, Saul," Jed called. He caught Beth's eye and gave a brief nod. There would be a round of sandwiches for Saul when Jed's food arrived. He knew Saul's pension didn't go far and the old man was good company.

"Be my pleasure, young 'un." Saul paused to give Marmite's head a good scratch before settling into the window seat. "This weather plays havoc with me rheumatism. Reckon there's more storms coming."

Jed stretched his legs out, careful to position them where no one would be in danger of tripping when they came in. "You're usually right, Saul. You do have a knack for the weather."

"Is the *Govenek* fully manned?"

"And womanned," Jed said. "If that's a word. We have two women on the crew now. And yes, the number of volunteers remains gratifyingly high. We've a good mix of veterans and greenhorns."

"Times be changing."

"Sure are." Jed gave Beth a smile as she arrived with two enormous plates of sandwiches garnished with enough salad that it could have made a meal in itself, and two bowls of hand-cut chunky chips doused in salt and vinegar.

"You extra hungry today, boy?" Saul's faded blue eyes twinkled.

"Seems like Beth doubled my order by mistake," Jed replied. "Help me out, would you, Saul?" Saul was far too proud to take charity and this was a ritual that played out between them with some regularity. "You'd be doing me a favor." He patted his flat stomach. "Can't be getting tubby."

"Well…as long as it's going spare." Saul tucked into the food with gusto. "Best crab sandwiches in the county."

"Can't argue with that." Jed attacked his own meal and for a while the two men ate in silence. At some point, Marmite put his head on Jed's knee, gazing at him with soulful brown eyes. Saul slipped him a chip. Jed pretended not to notice. Once the food was gone, down to the last crumb, Jed sipped his beer, letting the malty flavor roll across his taste buds. He did a bit of people watching, making a mental list of everyone he knew who might be able to help out with Jonty's auction.

"Still on the lookout for someone who rows on your side of the boat, young 'un?"

Jed gave Saul a sharp glance. "Round here, Saul, I could cast a trawler net and not pull in a single fish of the right species."

"True enough, but I hear tell you've set your sights on the painter from Cliff House." Saul winked.

"Jesus! Is nothing sacred around this place?" Jed swallowed more beer. "I had a five-minute conversation with him at Kelly's last night. That's all."

"Five minutes is all it takes for half the village to have you married off. Now that would be something— Polruthan's first gay wedding." Saul cackled into the remains of his pint. "Just make sure I get an invitation."

Jed shook his head. He gave Marmite, who was snoring under the table, a pat. "Come on, boy, time to get back to work." Marmite huffed his displeasure, but wriggled from beneath the furniture. He nudged a few customers aside then plonked himself on the doormat, completely blocking the exit. Jed went to the bar to leave his fish money with Beth. She would hand it over when one of the fishermen came in. Jed gave Saul a brief wave then nudged Marmite out of the door. A sea mist had descended and the air was damp. Jed could taste the salt on his lips as he walked. He caught himself checking his watch, counting the hours until he could go back to Kelly's to meet Jonty. The enigmatic young artist had definitely gotten under his skin.

Jed spent the rest of the day buried in work. He'd spent the last hour deciding whether or not to take the initiative with Jonty and his little head had overruled his brain. He couldn't wait until later that night to see Jonty again. They both had to eat so, under the pretext of discussing the auction, Jed had decided to invite him to dinner. When he made a mistake on a delicate piece of detailing, Jed gave up for the day. He closed up the workshop, took a shower to rinse off the sawdust then changed into a clean pair of jeans and a T-shirt he knew brought out the blue of his eyes.

"Fancy another walk, Marm?" When Jed walked into the kitchen, Marmite twitched an ear but didn't move from his position next to the Aga. "Let me rephrase that. Fancy a walk to Kelly's?" The dog bounced up like a puppy, quivering with excitement. "Thought that would get your lazy backside off the floor. We have to make a couple of other stops first." Jed shoved two potatoes in the Aga to bake. By the time he'd walked to Cliff House and back, they'd be done. Fish and vegetables wouldn't take long, then they could all go to Kelly's for dessert — he just had to get Jonty to comply.

A chill wind was blasting through the narrow lanes of Polruthan when Jed left the cottage. He'd thrown a fleece on over his shirt and wasn't too bothered by the cold. The uphill walk to Cliff House would soon warm him up. Marmite gave him a baleful glance when they turned away from the beach.

"We're going to Kelly's later, okay? Besides, you need the exercise or you're going to be the fattest dog in Cornwall." Marmite snuffled his objection to that comment and nosed Jed's thigh with enough force to shove him toward the adjoining wall. "Hey! Grumpy mutt. You should be glad I'm taking you at all. We have to make a good impression, so behave yourself." After that, Marmite stuck to Jed's heel, occasionally nosing after an interesting smell but never straying too far. Jed had the dog's leather lead in his pocket but he'd only need to use it if he spotted a cat before Marmite did. He turned along the lane leading to Cliff House. The imposing building was set slightly apart and had an uninterrupted sea view that had to be worth a small fortune. Jed didn't particularly like the house itself, which, though whitewashed, was still too gray for his taste. If it wasn't for the flower gardens that dropped in levels down the hillside, the place might even have been considered forbidding. He couldn't see a bell when he reached the front door so lifted the brass knocker. He let it drop and could hear the resulting bang echoing down the hallway within. Turning away from the door, he admired the view. It was too overcast for there to be much of a sunset but the clouds had a silver glow where they met the sea. Gulls wheeled and called above the harbor as the fishing boats prepared to set sail. Footsteps inside the house had Jed swiveling back to face the door. It opened just a crack, the security chain pulling taut.

"Yes?" Jonty sounded nervous.

"Jonty, it's Jed Curnow, remember? From last night."

"Oh! Oh, yes." There was a rattle then the door opened. Jonty was shirtless and barefoot. He wore a tatty pair of shorts, which might once have been a pair of jeans. There was a ripped pocket hanging from the front and Jed guessed it had nothing to do with fashion. There was a tantalizing glimpse of bare flesh peeking through the hole behind it. Jed gave Jonty a thorough and shameless examination from his slim calves and narrow hips to his flat belly and rosy nipples. There was a flush building on his skin and his teeth were firmly embedded in his lower lip.

"I've come to take you to dinner," Jed said. At the mention of dinner, Marmite's tail thumped the ground. "Oh, and this is Marmite. Say hello, boy." Marmite lifted a paw.

"Oh! He's gorgeous." Jonty shook the paw then gave Marmite a good scratch behind the ears. Marmite tried to push his way into the house.

"And he knows it," Jed said, grabbing Marmite's collar before he could move in. "So. Dinner. You and me." He made it a statement, not a question. "And you're shivering, so we should continue this conversation inside."

"Oh, yes. Come in."

The hallway was very warm so Jed stripped off his fleece.

Jonty peeked from beneath his lashes. "Um, why? I mean, why do you want to take me to dinner?"

"Why not?" Jed replied. "We both need to eat and you want to talk about the art auction."

"I don't… I mean, I can't… I'm not really dressed for eating out."

"You look pretty good to me." Jed grinned, holding back a leer. "But it is winter, so we can wait while you…find some clothes."

"I…" Jonty's eyes were huge and round. "I mean…"

"Get dressed, Jonty." Jed let a tone of command creep into his words, softening them with an encouraging smile.

"You best come through." Jonty retreated along the hall, his expression one of relief. "Make yourself at home and I'll go change. The kitchen is through there." He gestured to his right.

Marmite knew an invitation when he heard it. He also understood the word 'kitchen', so Jed allowed him to lead the way, tail wagging. The room proved to be ultra-modern, the walls lined with glossy white units. The work surfaces were white marble, as were the floor tiles. There was no clutter anywhere. It couldn't have been more different from Jed's kitchen, or less inviting. Jed shivered. The room didn't reflect Jonty's personality at all. The island in the middle of the room had two chrome and black leather stools pulled up to it. Jed parked his behind on one of them while Marmite slumped to the floor in an untidy pile.

"This boy needs some warmth in his life, Marm," Jed muttered. "He must be starved of affection holed up in this place with no family." Jed knew Jonty had few friends. He wasn't seen around the village that much and Jed had never noticed him in the Crusty Crab. From what he'd heard, Jonty was viewed as an eccentric hermit who kept to himself but was always polite when he did have cause to speak to the locals. Everyone knew of his past history but his present was something of a mystery. The way he'd reacted to Jed when he'd become more forceful was promising. Jed knew a natural submissive when he saw one. He was less convinced Jonty had any clue about his nature or what he needed.

Jed resisted the urge to explore the house because he didn't want to invade Jonty's privacy. He needed to gain his trust and he wasn't going to do that by poking his nose into Jonty's sanctuary. There would be plenty of time to find out why Jonty remained in such an unforgiving house. He leaned down and gave Marmite's ears a rub. "Not long now, boy." Footsteps sounded on the stairs then Jonty appeared in the kitchen doorway. He'd swapped his shorts for a pair of navy chinos topped with a cream Weird Fish hoodie.

He'd tied his hair back into a short tail, which served to highlight his defined cheekbones. Jed hadn't noticed the previous evening but Jonty's eyes were a beautiful shade of light green. With his white blond hair and pale skin, he seemed almost ghostly.

"Um…is this okay?" Jonty tangled his fingers in the hem of his top. He didn't meet Jed's eyes.

"Perfect. You might want to consider some shoes, though."

"Oh! Yes." Jonty blushed. "I never wear shoes in the house. Sometimes I forget until I step outside."

Jed followed him into the hall where Jonty shoved his feet into a pair of tattered Converse. He tied the laces into sloppy bows. "I'm ready. Um, where are we going?" He gave Marmite a pat as the dog shoved past him to nose at the door.

"To my place for the main course, then on to Kelly's for dessert." Jed made sure the statement was clear and uncompromising. He wasn't inviting debate. Jonty had no need to consider options or make a decision, he just had to agree.

"Okay." Jonty opened the door, letting Marmite go first. "Oh, does Marmite need to be on a lead?"

Jed fingered the coil of leather in his pocket, visualizing how Jonty might look with a collar around his slender neck. He gave himself a mental smack. It was far too soon for such thoughts. "Marmite's too lazy to run away. The only time he gets up any speed is around food or when he spots a cat willing to let him chase after it. Even if he does bolt, everyone in the village knows him. Someone will bring him home, probably after he's convinced them he's starving and in need of a snack."

Jonty giggled. It was the first time Jed had heard him laugh and he found he liked it.

"Everyone falls for the big puppy eyes. Marmite is a shameless flirt."

They followed the dog along the lane from Cliff House then turned downhill toward the sea.

"I like Kelly's," Jonty volunteered. "I'm not a very good cook and when I'm painting I forget to eat. I think Kelly has kept me alive over the last year. Nobody bothers me when I go there."

"Sounds like you need someone to take care of you," Jed said. "Do you have a girlfriend? Boyfriend?"

"No! I mean…I find it hard to talk to people. I prefer to be alone."

"You're talking to me."

"I am, aren't I?" Jonty sounded surprised. "You should know that if I did have someone, it would be a boy. A man."

"I thought so. I didn't want to assume."

"You still want to take me to dinner?"

"Oh yes." Jed lengthened his stride. "I definitely have an appetite tonight."

Chapter Four

Jonty snapped to a halt. He didn't think he'd misinterpreted Jed's somewhat suggestive comment and he was having a hard time processing the idea that a man, any man, let alone one as gorgeous as Jed, could possibly be interested in him. He scurried to catch up, hoping that Jed hadn't noticed the minor meltdown going on behind him. Jonty reached the relative security of Jed's side but close proximity didn't help slow the pace of his heartbeat. He opened his mouth to speak but then couldn't think of anything remotely intelligent to say so closed it again. A set of mini tornadoes were whirling round and round in his head, scrambling his thoughts. He half expected a flying cow to land in front of him at any moment. He'd seen *Twister* — there were always cows.

"You don't have to make conversation, Jonty. Relax. This is just dinner."

It's as if he knows what I'm thinking. Jonty envied Jed his calm confidence. He seemed so certain about his place in the world, unlike Jonty, who didn't fit in anywhere. He found himself stepping closer to Jed's side, which somehow felt like a safe haven.

"Uh, where do you live?" Jonty asked. It seemed sensible to know where they were going.

"I have a place just back from the quay," Jed said. "My workshop is attached. It used to be a fisherman's cottage and netting shed."

"Wow, those are the oldest houses in the village. They're really pretty. I've always meant to paint them someday."

"You'd be very welcome, though having you painting outside my windows might be a bit distracting. I could saw off a finger or something." Jed was completely straight-faced as he spoke but then he broke into a deep chuckle. "I'm a carpenter."

"I would hate for you to lose any important parts," Jonty said. His face heated. "I mean…well, that is…" Even in the dim light he could spot the twinkle of amusement in Jed's blue eyes. "I'll be shutting up now."

"Much as I'd like to see you dig an even bigger hole to stand in," Jed said, "we're here. Do you want to let someone know where you are?"

"Do I need to?"

Marmite gave a disdainful woof.

"Marmite seems to think not." Jed pushed open his front door. "I hereby swear not to molest you…this evening."

"I…oh… That's good, I guess." Jonty wasn't so sure. He'd quite like to know how it might feel to have Jed's big, work-roughened hands on his body, holding him down. His dick twitched—something that seemed to happen with alarming frequency around Jed.

"Come on in." Jed showed him into a cozy kitchen with an oak table at its center. There was a huge butler sink and an array of what looked like hand-finished units. Marmite, after taking a few noisy slurps from his water dish, flopped down in a dog bed next to the Aga. Jonty could feel the heat coming off the oven. He loved the room, which was the complete opposite of his own sterile, unwelcoming version.

"Grab a chair," Jed said. "Potatoes are already in the oven. The fish and veggies won't take long. You're not a vegetarian, are you?"

"No," Jonty replied. "I don't eat much meat. I love fish, though."

"We're having monkfish, freshly caught this morning."

Jonty watched, fascinated, as Jed poured a little oil into a skillet then laid two generous fillets on top. He threw fresh broccoli into a pan of water with a sprinkle of salt. He made cooking look easy.

"I can even manage to burn scrambled eggs," Jonty commented.

"Perhaps you need a few lessons."

Jonty wasn't sure if Jed was talking about cooking or something else. He fidgeted in his chair. "It sure smells good." His stomach growled. After a few more minutes of watching and admiring Jed's culinary prowess, Jonty was rewarded with a plate of food he couldn't wait to sink his fork into. Jed had heaped an unruly pile of cutlery on the table along with condiments and napkins.

"Don't wait for me, it'll get cold." Jed set a jug of water and two tumblers on the table.

Jonty didn't need to be told twice. His first mouthful of fish melted on his tongue. "Wow!" He was too busy eating to say anything further. Compliments would have to wait. He didn't stop until his plate was clear and he looked at it with regret.

"I'm afraid there aren't any seconds." Jed grinned. "But you can have as many desserts as you want once we get to Kelly's." Next to the Aga, Marmite twitched his tail.

"That is the best fish I've ever eaten, bar none," Jonty said. "I'll be tempted to eat here every night now you've given away your secret talent."

"You can eat here as often as you like. Of course, there will have to be payment." Jed put the crockery on the drainer in a neat pile.

"What kind of payment?" Jonty asked, nibbling on his bottom lip. Jed came to stand next to him and Jonty had to crane his neck to look up at him.

"For tonight, I'm going to charge one kiss."

As Jed leaned toward him, Jonty parted his lips. The response was entirely involuntary but he could no more stop it than he could protest. He held his breath and his heart pounded, then Jed's lips made contact. The kiss was fleeting and chaste, just the slightest connection. It still sent a thrill straight to Jonty's groin and, much to his utter humiliation, he moaned.

"The debt is settled," Jed pronounced.

Jonty's fingers strayed toward his lips. They felt different somehow, more sensitive and tingly. He had no words but he didn't need any because Jed's expression told Jonty he understood.

"The dishes can wait. Are you ready for pudding?" Jed asked.

Dazed, Jonty nodded. He managed to get to his feet, almost knocked over his chair, then staggered toward the door. Outside, the temperature had dropped, even though they'd only been inside a short while, and Jonty was glad of his thick sweater. He usually shied away from company but found he was quite happy to be going wherever Jed decided they should go. He knew deep in his marrow that Jed would take care of him. It wasn't that he disliked being around people. He just got so tongue-tied when they spoke to him. It was easier to be alone.

Kelly's was the usual warm, glowing hubbub of noise and music. In the still of the night Jonty fancied the place had an almost magical quality — a little bubble of life protected from the sea mist and the crashing waves by the sheer energy it contained. As they approached, he began to feel a bit anxious. It was one thing coming on his own and hiding in a corner. It was another thing entirely to be arriving with Jed who seemed to know everyone in the village right down to the last hamster. His steps faltered.

"You okay?" Jed slowed his steps until Jonty caught up with him again.

"I'm not sure this is a good idea." Jonty was torn — he wanted to spend time with Jed but not in a crowd.

"Dessert is *always* a good idea. Have you ever tried Kelly's Peach Melba? He makes it with baked peaches, clotted cream vanilla ice cream and homemade raspberry syrup."

"It's just… I mean…"

"Hey, stop worrying." Jed put his arm around Jonty's shoulders. "You're trembling."

"Sorry." Jonty wanted to run and hide but he found himself leaning toward Jed's warmth.

"We'll get dessert to go. Take it back to my place."

"You don't mind?"

"Mind having you all to myself? Not at all." Jed's grin was disarming.

"Then the Peach Melba sounds spectacular." The tension eased from Jonty's frame but he was glad Jed didn't move his arm. Marmite whined.

"Marm is getting impatient. You want to wait out here or come in with me?"

"I'll come in. Sorry to be such a wuss."

"Stop putting yourself down. You are who you are and not everyone wants to be surrounded by people. Hey, I work alone all day and have conversations with my dog, so we make the perfect pair."

Jonty giggled. "Marmite seems like a good listener."

"Well, he doesn't argue much. Come on, the sooner we get in there, the sooner we can leave." Marmite was already nosing at the door. He used his snout to shove it open. "Incoming," Jed shouted, following close behind, Jonty firmly tucked against his side.

"Hiya, Jed. Jonty." Kelly banged on the counter and the hubbub subsided. "Anyone in here dogaphobic?" Kelly yelled. "Cos Marmite's a better customer than the rest of you layabouts put together so if you're gonna start sneezing it's time for you to leave."

"Kelly makes the exact same announcement every time I bring Marmite in," Jed said. "Because he knows everyone will want to order extra so they can give the mutt treats."

Sure enough a queue formed. Almost everyone ordered one of Kelly's 'special' biscuits alongside whatever they were having.

"He doesn't charge for the biscuits. He makes enough from all the extra drinks."

Marmite wriggled his way between the tables, resting his chin on various thighs, accepting ear scratches with magnanimity. Each biscuit he was offered he accepted with delicate snuffles.

"He's shameless!" Jonty exclaimed.

"He believes he was born with those big brown eyes for good reason," Jed replied. "You should see him around lady dogs. Now how about we order so we can get out of here?"

"It's okay," Jonty said. "We can stay. I'd hate to deprive Marmite of his treats and now we're in here, I just feel stupid."

Jed beamed. He ordered desserts and hot chocolate then led Jonty to a side table next to a window. "As soon as you've had enough, just say." He pulled out a chair. "Take a seat."

"Such a gentleman."

Jed pulled another chair close. He sat, resting his hand on Jonty's thigh. "Good manners cost nothing."

Jonty placed his smaller hand on top of Jed's, noting the contrast between Jed's tan and his own paler skin. "Strong hands."

"Years of working with wood."

"Do you think you'll be able to do something in wood for the auction?" Jonty asked. "I don't know what kind of carpentry you do. Is it mostly furniture?"

"I do a lot of bespoke pieces but I like to carve as well," Jed said. "I use driftwood from the beach and if someone in the village is having a tree felled they usually give me first pickings, so I have plenty of material. I'd love to do something for the auction."

"That sounds great."

Their conversation was interrupted when Kelly arrived with their order. He gave their hands a pointed glance. "You two getting along then?"

Jonty's face heated. He yanked his hand away and shuffled his chair a few inches from Jed's."

"Hey, I liked that hand right where it was." Jed grabbed it, intertwining their fingers.

Kelly chuckled. He unloaded his tray before leaving them without further comment. Jed rolled his eyes. "Kelly fancies himself a matchmaker. He introduced us so he thinks that gives him a God-given right to know our business from now on. I can guarantee you I'll get a call tomorrow asking for details."

"Sounds like my sister. I mean—how she used to be before she…" Jonty couldn't bring himself to say the word 'died'. "Every time I hooked up with a guy she wanted to know everything and if she and I were out together…she'd pick out potential boyfriends for me and give them marks out of ten."

"Think I'd make a ten?" Jed asked.

"You'd be off the chart." *Oh God, did I say that out loud?*

"Good to know."

Jed's smirk was the sexiest thing Jonty had seen in a long time. He spooned ice cream into his mouth in the hope that the cold would somehow filter toward his overheated groin. "We should talk about the auction."

"A change of subject might be advisable." Jed smiled and the lines at the sides of his eyes crinkled.

Jonty swallowed more ice cream. *Perhaps I should dump the bowl in my lap.* "I need to start talking to more local artists so they have time to prepare but I don't know enough people. I mean, I know who some of them are but not to talk to."

"It won't be a problem. They'll all know who *you* are."

"They will?" Jonty frowned. "Oh, because of what happened? I don't want anyone doing this out of sympathy." He pushed his ice cream away, feeling a bit sick. "Perhaps this isn't such a good idea."

"I didn't mean to upset you." Jed leaned toward him. Jonty could smell the light scent of his aftershave. It made his head spin.

"You didn't."

"I did and I'm sorry, but the auction is a fantastic idea. People will understand why you want to mark the anniversary and say thank you to the people who saved your life."

"I suppose I thought I could just raise some money and no one would think about what happened a year ago."

"It was big news around here, Jonty. There's no avoiding it, especially if you want to get some media coverage. The papers will play that angle, no doubt."

Jonty extracted his hand from Jed's hold. "I haven't thought this through at all. I'm such an idiot. I can't..." He shoved his chair back. "I need some air."

"Okay." There was no hint of impatience in Jed's tone. He gave a short, sharp whistle. Marmite, who was chomping on yet another biscuit under someone else's table, pricked up his ears. "Time to go home, Marm." Tail wagging, Marmite weaved his way through tables and chairs to sit in front of the exit.

Jonty kept his head down as he and Jed followed the dog outside. The crisp air was shocking and Jonty shivered. Jed put an arm around his shoulders, pulling him close. It was as if he'd been wrapped in a blanket of warmth and protection. Jonty knew he should move away, take care of himself, but he couldn't. He snuggled against Jed all the way to Cliff House.

"Get yourself to bed, Jonty. Stay warm. Everything will be clearer in the morning." Jed helped him fit his key in the lock then gave him a gentle nudge inside. Marmite gave his hand a soggy slurp.

"I'm sorry…"

"You have nothing to apologize for. I had a great evening. I hope we can do it again sometime soon?"

"Are you asking me on another date?" Jonty couldn't quite believe Jed would want to see him again.

"Perhaps I shouldn't ask. I'll just tell you." Jed grinned. "Then all you have to do is be…obedient."

Jonty shivered and this time it wasn't from the cold. "Thank you for dinner, Jed." Jonty rose on his toes in order to give Jed a light kiss on the cheek. Shocked at his own bravery, he slipped into the hall, pushing the door closed behind him. He leaned on it, taking deep gulps of air. "Oh my God, what have I done?" Playing with fire almost always ended in burns and Jonty had just poured fuel on flames he had no hope of controlling. He dashed up the stairs to his bedroom, tearing off his clothes as he went. He dived beneath the duvet, yanking it over his head like a small child hiding from the monster under the bed. His heart pounded. He tucked his knees to his chest, curling around his anxiety.

Since the yachting tragedy, not a day went by when Jonty didn't question each decision he'd made during that fateful voyage. He relived every second of the horror over and over in his dreams. He'd almost come to terms with the circumstances of his father's death — the post mortem had concluded massive hemorrhaging from a head injury had killed Rex — which had been a stupid accident. He hadn't forgiven him for leaving the rest of the family to deal with the mess he'd led them into. If only Rex had swallowed his pride and turned back when Jonty had suggested it, then his mother and

Evie might still be alive. His mum was a different matter. Jonty couldn't help but think that had he been a better sailor, it might have been him standing beneath the mast when it had fallen. Instead, the image of his mother's crushed form would remain with him forever. He'd been told that her body couldn't be retrieved until after the *Caroline* had been towed back to shore.

He had little memory of the time after he and Evie had gone below. He remembered Evie being hurt after the boat rolled and trying to keep them both out of the water that sloshed around them. He'd lost consciousness for several hours and when he'd woken, he'd been holding his sister's dead body in his arms. Hypothermia had made thinking difficult but somehow he'd made it onto the deck where he'd fired the second flare. He didn't recall anything after that — he'd remained unconscious throughout the rescue, waking in Plymouth Hospital the following day. The kindly police sergeant who'd come to visit him told him he'd fallen into the sea. He'd been just minutes from death.

"I can't let this beat me." Jonty shoved the duvet away. *No more hiding.* He wanted his life back. Kissing Jed felt like the first step toward something new and good. It was time to make some new memories to replace the nightmares.

Chapter Five

Jonty spent the rest of the night painting and, as dawn broke, he still bubbled with energy. Paint splattered his hands and clothes. He picked at a dried lump of cerulean stuck to a knuckle then gave up. He liked the color anyway. Inspired by the clear quality of the morning light, he grabbed a sketchpad and some pencils, shoved them into a satchel along with a bottle of water and a wizened, yellow apple, then searched out his comfiest deck shoes from the back of the hall cupboard. Outside, the air was crisp with a nip of frost but Jonty didn't feel the cold. He trotted downhill toward the bay, eager to put pencil to paper.

For such an early hour, there was a lot of activity around the village. Jonty passed three dog walkers, one being towed along by an enormous Great Dane, the others more in control of their much smaller pets. Enticing smells issued from the bakery where the front door was propped open by a lobster pot. Down on the quay, two fishing boats were moored, their catches being unloaded. *I should have come down here sooner!* Jonty settled on a corner of the harbor wall where he could see the quay, the oldest cottages and the lifeboat station. Behind him, waves rolled onto the shore and the beach stretched into the distance. After a brief glance, he kept his gaze fixed on the bustle of the harbor. It was one thing to paint the sea from behind the windows of Cliff House, quite another to do it up close and personal. Jonty counted it a win that he could sit as close as he did.

His first target was the row of ancient, pastel-colored cottages, set back from the quay. There was such a great mixture of textures and not a straight wall or roofline among them. He sketched with sure, rapid strokes, wishing he'd thought to bring some colored pencils or watercolors. He'd have to come back to capture the rainbow hues and subtle nuances of the light. Engrossed, he flicked over to a clean sheet and turned to draw the fishermen on the jetty, the eager seagulls lined up nearby in hope of scraps. He filled page after page with busy images—a volunteer opening the lifeboat station, struggling to heave the collection bin outside—the butcher's apprentice cycling toward the village center, head bent over his handlebars—a fat ginger cat sitting on a wall giving his whiskers a wash. Everywhere he looked there was more inspiration and gradually an idea for a series of small watercolors formed in his mind. He'd call the series *Village Life* and put them into the auction. He chewed the end of his pencil, fixing the progression of images in his mind. He was so distracted that when someone touched his knee, he almost fell backward off the wall.

"Hey now, you don't want to be falling down there."

Jonty found himself hauled forward by his sweater. Heart pounding, he tilted his head back to find Jed Curnow grinning down at him. Something wet washed across his hand. Marmite had given him a slurp and was now nuzzling his thigh.

"You were off with the fairies, weren't you? Sorry I startled you."

"I…" Jonty peered over the sheer drop behind him. He swallowed, feeling a little lightheaded. If he had fallen, he would likely have cracked his skull and broken a few bones. A sleepless night and no breakfast wasn't a good combination for thinking straight, or apparently for standing. He shuffled off the wall but his knees gave way. Jed caught him and he was surrounded with warm strength. With safety. He considered pulling away and dismissed it as a stupid idea.

"Have you been up all night, Jonty?"

Jonty scuffed the toe of his sneaker on the ground. "I…umm…maybe? I was painting."

"And have you eaten anything this morning?"

"I brought an apple."

"An apple."

Jonty got disgusted looks from both Jed and Marmite. He giggled. "I *am* kind of hungry and my butt hurts." He rubbed at his arse, which had gone to sleep on the cold stone wall and was now tingling.

"You're killing me." Jed gazed skyward as if seeking divine intervention. "You're coming back to my place. You should not be allowed out on your own without a minder."

Jonty wondered if Jed might be available for the position. If it meant being escorted around the village with Jed's strong arm around his shoulder, he could live with it. He gave less than a second's thought to what other people might think as Jed guided him the two hundred yards to his home, which was one of the picture postcard properties Jonty had been drawing. It was on the end of the row, painted pale blue, and had a large workshop to one side—details Jonty hadn't noticed in the dark the previous evening.

"We'll go in round the back." Jed indicated the gate. "Marm didn't get into the water this morning but I don't want him tracking dirt through the house." Marmite knew the routine and was soon scarfing down his breakfast from a caldron-sized bowl.

"He has quite an appetite," Jonty said, settling in a comfortable, curved-back chair stuffed with cushions.

"We had a long walk this morning, but he'd eat all day if I let him. He's a big dog, but he's lazy. He'd be fat as a house if I didn't force exercise on him."

"Why's he called Marmite?" Jonty asked. "I mean, I get the color, but is that the only reason?"

"To start with I called him Bigfoot. When he was a puppy, his paws were way too big for him. He was clumsy as heck, but curious too. I left the grocery bags on the floor one day and he got into them while I was in the bathroom. There was stuff everywhere and the jar of Marmite had smashed on the flagstones. He rolled in it and I can tell you that sticky stuff and puppy fur do not go together. He was covered in it. There were Marmite paw prints everywhere. I had to bathe him three times. He's three years old now and I swear I still find bits of it when I clean."

Jonty chuckled. "He must have been a gorgeous puppy."

"Far too adorable for his own good." Jed was staring at Jonty, not the dog.

Heat crept up Jonty's neck to his cheeks. He wasn't sure where to look but kept getting drawn back to Jed's blue eyes. He ran his tongue along his bottom lip, remembering the brief kiss he'd given Jed the previous evening. His stomach rumbled then he followed that up with a yawn. *Way to make a good impression, Jonty. Go you!*

Laughing, Jed turned to the stove. "I'm going to feed you, then I'm going to wrap you up in a fleecy blanket and let you catch up on some sleep. I whip up a mean pancake—does that sound okay?"

"I haven't had pancakes for ages. I'd love some."

"Then that is what you will have."

Jonty watched Jed as he whisked a batch of batter then ladled it into a hot pan. The smell was tantalizing and Jonty realized how much his belly ached. He was tempted to sit there, poised with knife and fork in hand so that he could eat as soon as a pancake hit his plate, but he had to wait while Jed piled his stack with chopped banana and drizzled the lot with maple syrup.

"You go ahead," Jed ordered, waving a spatula at him. "Mine won't take a minute."

It wasn't long before they both sat munching happily. Marmite opened one eye but didn't move.

"He doesn't like pancakes?" Jonty asked around a mouthful of food.

"We're safe. If we were eating b-a-c-o-n"—Jed spelled the word out—"he'd be drooling all over us by now. He's a shameless beggar when he wants something."

"I'd beg for these pancakes," Jonty said. "They're wonderful."

"I'd like to see that."

Jonty swallowed. He had a sudden image of getting on his knees for Jed, pleading to be allowed to suck him.

If his cock was in proportion, it must be magnificent. Jonty's breath stuttered and he covered his embarrassment by shoving a final fork load of pancake into his mouth. He glanced at Jed from beneath his lashes. Jed's expression said that he knew exactly what Jonty was thinking.

"Thank you for breakfast." Jonty laid his cutlery carefully on the empty plate. "I think I should be getting home." He didn't want to go. Jed's kitchen was warm and cozy. Jed was…Jed. Strong, safe, in control.

"No."

"No?" Jonty's cheeks warmed.

"No. I'm putting you to bed here. You're half asleep now. If you stagger up that hill with your eyes closed you'll end up flat on your face, then roll all the way back to the harbor."

"I don't want to be any trouble." Jonty nibbled his lower lip. A wave of fatigue washed over him. *Perhaps I could just sleep here in this chair.*

"Come on, I'll show you the bedroom."

Jed kept close behind him all the way up the narrow staircase, as if he was afraid Jonty might fall.

"First door on the left."

Jonty pushed the door open to find a room just as welcoming as the kitchen. It was simply furnished and had waxed floorboards covered by colorful rugs rather than carpet. The walls were plastered and painted soft, mossy green. There were shutters at the windows rather than curtains and Jed pulled them closed, darkening the room.

"The bathroom is just across the landing if you need it. I changed the sheets yesterday…"

Jonty admired the bed, brass bed head and footer both gleaming. A thick duvet was topped by a bright blue knitted blanket.

"There may be the odd dog hair…"

"Is this your room, Jed?"

Jed nodded. "I use the spare as an office and there are a few free weights in there. You'll be more comfortable if you take your clothes off. I'll give you some privacy." Jed slipped from the room, moving quietly for such a big man.

Jonty stroked the bedcover. The whole room was warm and inviting, the bed so tempting. He kicked off his shoes and socks, dropped his trousers then removed his pullover. He kept his T-shirt and underwear on even though he was accustomed to sleeping naked. He slipped beneath the duvet, which surrounded him in a soft cloud of comfort. The pillows were cool against his cheek but soon warmed. His muscles relaxed, tension he didn't know was there seeping from his body. There was a soft knock at the door then Jed appeared, Marmite nosing past him.

"How are you doing?" Jed asked.

"I'm good. Really good. Thanks." Jonty burrowed deeper beneath the duvet. "It's so comfy in here."

"Sleep. Marm wants to be here—is that okay?"

"Sure. Does he snore?" Jonty giggled. His eyes were already drifting closed.

"Yep, but he seems to want to keep watch."

Jonty slipped his arm from under the covers. He reached down to touch Marmite's soft head. "Feel safe here…" Then sleep claimed him.

* * * *

Jed pulled the bedroom door partway closed. Marmite would be able to nose his way out if he wanted to, but he was already snoring and wouldn't be moving for a while. Jed was a bit jealous that the dog got to stay and keep Jonty company while he slept instead of him, but he had to be content with having Jonty safely tucked up in his bed. He had to work and Jonty needed rest.

It was a bit strange in the workshop without Marmite propping open the door. Jed turned on the radio for company. He had some paperwork to get done before he could begin the part of his job he loved, working with wood. While he sorted invoices and paid bills, he thought about what he might make for Jonty's auction. He had a lovely piece of teak he'd been saving to make into a group of nesting bowls and a gorgeous block of cherry that would make a fantastic jewel casket, but neither seemed right. He wanted to produce something more artistic and abstract. Inspiration would come, probably when he least expected it.

He sketched some designs for the set of garden furniture on his order list, finished repairing an oak rocking chair then laid out some seasoned beech destined to become a bookcase. When he checked the time, it was past midday and his stomach was growling its displeasure. He rubbed a few kinks out of his lower back, brushed the sawdust from his trousers then made his way through to the house. There would be no visit to the Crusty Crab, not with Jonty resting upstairs. Jed wouldn't dream of leaving him alone.

Before he reached the kitchen, Jed detected the aroma of something cooking. His mouth watered and it only got worse when he found Jonty, barefoot and dressed just in a T-shirt and jeans, dancing and singing in front of the stove. Marmite was stretched out by the Aga, his tail bashing the floor in time with Jonty's rhythm. It wasn't the most tuneful singing Jed had ever heard, but it was enthusiastic. He cleared his throat and Jonty whirled around. A few drops of something flew from the end of the spoon he was holding and landed across the front of Jed's shirt. Jonty's eyes grew huge and his mouth opened. He gasped. "Oh no! I'm so sorry!"

Jed found himself assaulted with a wet cloth wielded by Jonty, which only served to make the mess on his clothes worse.

"I found a container of soup in the fridge and I thought even I could manage to heat it up without setting fire to anything," Jonty babbled, "but now I've made you all sticky. I'm hopeless."

Jed took a gentle hold of Jonty's wrist before steering him to a seat by the table. "It's just a shirt, Jonty. It'll soon wash and I appreciate you making me lunch. The soup smells great." He stripped off his shirt, putting it aside to throw in the washing machine later.

"Oh…" Jonty made a peculiar little moaning sound.

"Are you okay?" Puzzled, Jed examined Jonty's face. His eyes were bright, his cheeks flushed. "You're not getting a fever, are you?"

"I'm fine." Jonty's voice was a touch higher pitched than usual.

"Why don't you serve the soup while I get a fresh shirt?"

"Do you have to? Oh—I didn't mean to say that out loud." Jonty found something interesting on the floor to stare at but his gaze rose in increments until it was fixed on Jed's bare chest once more.

Jed chuckled. Every now and again he got a glimpse of how Jonty must have been before tragic circumstances subdued his natural exuberance. Jed guessed he might have a brat on his hands, albeit one hidden beneath defensive layers. "Like what you see, huh?" He flexed a little, teasing. Jonty had a tea towel positioned over his groin but it wasn't doing much to conceal his arousal. Jed made sure to brush against him when he passed. Jonty squeaked and back-pedaled toward the sink where he ran the cold tap and splashed some water on his face. Jed laughed all the way to the bedroom, delighted at Jonty's reaction. He changed, putting on a T-shirt that had shrunk a bit in the wash and now fitted like a second skin. It would be fun to keep Jonty a little on edge.

Making sure he didn't startle Jonty, Jed made some noise as he re-entered the kitchen. "There, all clean and ready to eat."

Jonty was still a bit pink. His sleep-tousled hair had escaped its band and fell around his shoulders in a blond curtain. He'd sawn up a loaf of bread into big chunks and the soup had been ladled into bowls. Jed pulled up a chair, grabbed a spoon then tucked in. "It's so nice to have lunch made for me," he said, between spoonfuls. "I usually head for the Crab."

"I've never been in there," Jonty said.

"They do the most amazing crab sandwiches. I'll take you one day."

"Like, on a date?" Jonty batted his lashes.

"Yes, Jonty. On a date."

"So everyone knows you're…"

"Gay? Well, I don't broadcast the fact, but once one person knows something around here, the entire village knows."

"I wasn't sure at first…I can never tell…but I'm glad."

Jed quirked an eyebrow. "So does that mean you'll let me take you out?"

"Do I have a choice?" Jonty affected wide-eyed innocence.

"You can respond with 'yes, Jed' or 'yes, Sir' — that's a choice." Jed held his breath. He had no idea how Jonty might react or if he'd gone too far.

"Yes, Sir?" Jonty's response was little more than a whisper and had a hint of a question. His lips held the trace of a smile, which sent waves of deep satisfaction through Jed's body.

"Is that an answer or a question?" The moment was broken by a loud and persistent beeping.

"What's that?" Jonty glanced around. Marmite sat up, suddenly attentive.

"My pager." Jed took it from his pocket to check the message. "I have to go. The lifeboat has been called out." He grabbed a fleece from the back of the kitchen door. "Do you mind staying here to look after Marmite? I don't know how long I'll be."

"Of course."

"If you need to be somewhere else, just take him to Kelly's. His food's under the sink — fill the measuring cup and mix it with some water. He eats around six-thirty." Jed had one hand on the doorknob, reluctant to leave.

"Go!" Jonty frowned. "Marmite and I will be just fine. People need you."

"See you later." Jed ran for the boatshed, cursing his luck that an important moment with Jonty had been interrupted. His fellow volunteers were converging on the lifeboat station and Jed had to put thoughts of Jonty aside but it made him feel warm inside that he had a special someone to come back to as well as his dog.

Chapter Six

When the door closed behind Jed, all the air in Jonty's lungs escaped in a rush. He leaned back in his chair, overwhelmed by the last few minutes. Jed had asked him out, which was wonderful, but he'd asked in such a way that heated Jonty's blood. He'd revealed himself to be what Jonty had already guessed, a Dominant — or at the very least dominant with a small 'd'. That knowledge did things to parts of Jonty's body that made him squirm but before he'd been able to give a proper, straightforward answer, Jed had run off into God knew what kind of danger.

"Damn it. Why couldn't I just answer without making it a question, Marmite?" The big dog ambled over to rest his chin on Jonty's thigh. Jonty gave him a scratch behind the ears, eliciting happy snuffles. "Yes, that's exactly how I feel. Seems your master is a Master in more ways than one, huh?" Marmite nudged against his hand, demanding more attention. "So, what are we going to do for the rest of the day to stop me worrying about Jed?" It was a serious question. Jonty couldn't help but think about all the possible scenarios that might play out at sea. His own nightmares still haunted him and the thought of losing someone else he was beginning to care deeply about made his skin itch.

Clearing up in the kitchen didn't take long enough, even with the added obstacle of having to climb over Marmite every time he wanted to get to the sink. Jonty needed a distraction. "Perhaps it's time to look up some local artists," he mumbled. "Fancy a walk, Marmite? If I take you with me, people are bound to talk to me, aren't they?"

Marmite gave a low bark and scrambled to his feet.

"Question is, do I need a lead? I know Jed doesn't use one with you." Jonty guessed that if Marmite wanted to run, he could tow him along without difficulty. Marmite wandered across the kitchen. He thrust his head into a basket of soft toys then returned with a lead in his mouth, making Jonty chuckle. "Okay then. I guess that answers my question." Jonty clipped the lead to Marmite's collar. As he touched the worn leather, his fingers strayed to his throat and he wondered what it might feel like to have leather wrapped around it. He shivered, worried that he liked the idea a bit too much. As if sensing Jonty's need for air, Marmite moved toward the door. Jonty followed, grateful the dog was so perceptive. Then he realized he wasn't properly dressed and needed shoes.

"Good grief, I'm hopeless." He shook his head. "Wait there, Marm. I won't be long." He trotted upstairs to Jed's bedroom. While he finished dressing, he stared at the bed — the most comfortable he could ever remember sleeping in. The brass rails were no longer innocuous. He could imagine how it might feel to be bound to them, helpless, spread wide while Jed touched him any way he pleased with his big, work-calloused hands. A whimper escaped Jonty's lips. He was getting hard. He debated a trip to the bathroom for some relief but instead opted to splash his face with cold water and think deflating thoughts. A bark of inquiry from downstairs got him moving and soon he and Marmite were strolling toward the quay.

Jonty gave Marmite plenty of slack and let him take the lead. He made a beeline for the lifeboat station and, though Jonty felt a little anxious about visiting, he followed. The boat doors were open, the interior of the cavernous space empty. Jonty glanced out to sea but the boat wasn't visible even as an orange dot on the horizon. He put some loose change from his pocket into the collection bin, watching the coins roll in a spiral toward a small hole. It reminded him of a whirlpool.

"Hey, thanks for the donation!"

Jonty peered inside the dark interior of the shed, trying to see who had spoken. Hobbling toward him on crutches was a young man about his own age, with a wide grin on his face.

"You're welcome. It wasn't much."

"Every penny counts. I'm Steve Bower." The young man secured his crutch beneath an arm then held out a hand. He wobbled and for a moment Jonty thought he might overbalance. He gave the offered hand a quick shake.

"Please don't fall over!"

Marmite tugged at his lead and Jonty almost went down too.

"Seems like neither of us is very good at staying upright at the moment." Steve's grin was infectious and Jonty relaxed. "Hey, Marmite, you missing Jed?"

Marmite nudged Steve's knee, almost causing another catastrophe. "You can let him off the lead if you like. He has a water dish inside and there's a bowl of biscuits, which I'm sure he can smell from here."

Jonty shrugged. He unclipped the lead and Marmite disappeared into the boatshed, tail wagging with sheer joy.

"You're Jonty Trelawn." It was a statement not a question. "From Cliff House. So are you and Jed…"

"Friends. We're friends!"

"Ooookay." Steve chuckled. "Well, Jed's friend—just so you know, you'll be breaking the heart of every gay man within a fifty-mile radius if you get past the 'friend' stage."

"I…I mean… Do you…" Jonty's tongue wasn't working.

"Good Lord, no." Steve laughed. "I'm engaged to the coxswain's daughter, Rose Poldean. She'd have my balls if I so much as glanced at anyone else, male or female."

Jonty was relieved. He didn't like the idea that Jed had other admirers even though common sense told him that had to be the case. Jed was gorgeous. It was a miracle he was still single.

"I hear you're planning a fundraiser for the boat. You want to come in for a look around? Have a cuppa with me?"

"Only if you have time…"

"It's all I have at the moment. I'm off work because of the leg so I'm making myself useful helping out here. I'd love some company." Steve led the way inside. "I'll give you a quick tour."

The biggest space in the shed was, of course, for the boat and the rails that let it slide into the water. There was a huge hoist to drag it back into place.

"You should come and watch next time there's a shout. It's dramatic when the boat hits the water on the way out."

"I can imagine." Jonty thought that might make a good picture.

"This is the kit room." Walls peppered with pegs held bright yellow over-trousers and coats. Yellow boots were lined up beneath in neat pairs. Several pegs were empty. Jonty scanned the name tags until he found Jed's and then his locker, in a bank against the window wall.

"Through there's the shower room. The two girls always get to go first—we only have shared facilities here. Women on the team is quite a new thing. The big lockers hold specialist kit like dry suits for the swimmers, flippers, masks. Helmets are on the shelf."

"There are a lot."

"We have enough trained volunteers for three crews," Steve replied. "Some people can only be on call on certain days because of their jobs. Others, like Jed and my father-in-law to be, are more flexible. Serious shouts mean the most experienced crew gets called out. Jed's on stand-down one week in three but he keeps his pager on even then because he's deputy coxswain and a rescue swimmer. Sometimes there's no one else to replace him."

"Wow. I had no idea he was such an integral part of all this." Jonty made a note to have a discussion with Jed about taking care of himself.

"I'm a volunteer too," Steve said. "When I'm in one piece that is. But my day job is with the police force so

I'm not often available. I'm still learning the ropes. A lot of men on the crew had fathers and grandfathers involved — it's a family tradition." He followed a corridor to a spacious break room where he put the kettle on. Marmite was reclined on a blanket in the corner, looking for all the world like he owned the place.

"Settled in for the long haul, Marm?" Jonty said, amused.

"Some nights we have three or four dogs in here. Marmite is a big favorite. How do you take your tea?"

"Milky please," Jonty replied. "Quite weak. Just wave a tea bag in the general direction of the cup."

"Wow. Don't say that too loud when the crew are in here. Weak tea is against the law. Most of them drink it so strong the spoon stands upright."

Jonty accepted a mug then sat at the table. He sipped his drink while Steve produced a plate of biscuits. "On rough nights, the families gather in here. Wives, girlfriends, boyfriends, sometimes kids. Waiting is the hardest part of a call-out."

"Is Rose on the crew?"

"No. She's an events manager and works away a lot, sometimes abroad. She can't commit the time. She does embroidery in her spare time — I know she'd love to contribute something to your auction."

"How do you know about that?" Jonty asked, intrigued.

"You're the talk of the village." Steve chuckled. "Famous but reclusive artist with a tragic past decides to support our little boat…oh, I'm so sorry. My mouth runs away from me sometimes. Rose is gonna kick my arse."

"Your behind is safe." Jonty shrugged. "I can't get away from what happened. People round here all know about it. Heck, someone on the crew pulled me out of the water."

"Don't you know who it was?"

Jonty wrapped his hands around his warm mug. "No and it doesn't matter. The whole crew saved my life, not one man. Or woman."

"I'm still sorry. It was insensitive and I should know better."

"I like that you're not walking on eggshells around me." Jonty grinned. "I need a friend who says what he thinks and calls me out when I'm being a prat."

"You have a deal, providing you promise to do the same. I'm a policeman. People can be careful around me too. Apart from Rose. That woman is scary." He rolled his eyes.

"Wuss."

"Not denying it. Now tell me more about this auction you're planning."

Jonty outlined his plans. "So you see, I need introductions. I'd love a contribution from Rose."

"Count her in. I'm afraid I don't have a creative bone in my body but as a copper I do know who's where on my beat. There's a converted barn out on the main road shared by a glassblower and a blacksmith—husband and wife team. Then Molly Caine is a potter. She has a small studio in the next village. The vicar at All Saints, fondly known around here as Trev the Rev, does some watercolors in his spare time."

"He came to see me after… Well, I wasn't very nice to him," Jonty said.

"I'm pretty sure forgiveness is in his job description. He'd love to help. If you want, we can split the list. I'll drum up support from some and you can do a few others."

"I'd really appreciate that. Jed knows some people too and I'm going to hit up friends from London. I want there to be a good mix of lots, so more people are interested in bidding. If I can find someone good with web stuff, we could even have a web page. I think online bidding might be going a bit far."

"That's a brilliant idea. Someone could make a Facebook page for you too. I think Callum works in IT — he's out on the boat at the moment — I'll ask when they get back."

"Can I ask what the call was about?"

"Call from a freighter with an injured crewman. Not serious enough to drag the flyboys out. The guy's walking wounded apparently."

"So not too dangerous?"

"Every call has its dangers, Jonty. Small boat alongside big boat in heavy seas, not a great combo, but they're well trained. They'll be fine. It's going to be a late one, though. The coastguard will ring through when they're due back. They'll have an ambulance waiting for the patient. I doubt it will be much before midnight."

Jonty checked his watch — it wasn't even four o' clock. "Well, in that case I'm going to pay a visit to the guy who makes stained glass in that place next to the butcher's. Are you going to be here later?"

"Yep. The crew will want feeding when they get back. I'm in for the long haul."

"Can I come back later and wait with you?"

"Sure, that would be great. There's a TV. We can watch bad movies while we wait."

"Perfect. Marmite, time to move." Marmite twitched one ear. "I think he's related to a giant sloth," Jonty muttered.

"You're welcome to leave him here. He'll be fine and I'd like the company."

"Okay. I'll never be able to drag him anywhere he doesn't want to go. He's the size of a grizzly bear. I'll be back with his dinner by half past six. If I'm not, he might decide to eat you instead."

Steve fell about laughing. "Underneath that quiet, shy thing you have going on, there's quite the sense of humor. Friends or not, Jed's going to have his hands full with you, isn't he?"

God, I hope so. Jonty waved goodbye and headed into the village.

* * * *

Jonty needn't have worried about introducing himself to someone he'd never met. Chester Carling, the stained glass maker, acted as if they'd been friends for years and didn't hesitate to offer up a beautiful sun catcher for the auction. Jonty also bought a small panel depicting a sunset over the waves that he planned to give Jed as a gift — a thank you for his help. He turned down a coffee at Chester's then headed back to Jed's to collect Marmite's supper. He found a Tupperware box in a cupboard, using it to hold two large scoops of pellets. He made a mental note of how much water he needed to add, picked up one of Marmite's toys then made his way the short distance back to the lifeboat station. The collection bin had disappeared and the main doors had been pulled shut but a side door stood open and a warm glow came from inside.

"Steve?" Jonty called.

"In here."

Jonty followed the sound of Steve's voice and found him in the kitchen-cum-common room chopping vegetables.

"Hey, welcome back."

Jonty staggered as Marmite used his head as a battering ram against a thigh before proceeding to lick him and make happy snuffles.

"Someone's glad to see you."

"More like he knows who has his supper." Jonty dropped to his knees and gave Marmite a hug. "I just have to mix it up, boy. It won't be long." Marmite shoved him over then slurped his face. "Ugh! Get off of me!" Jonty couldn't stop giggling. "How can I make your dinner if I'm down here?" He grabbed Steve's hand and was hauled to his feet. "Wow. Thanks. That dog's a menace."

"Thinks with his stomach," Steve said. "Maybe you should feed him now?"

Jonty mixed the dog food, using a metal bowl that Steve produced. He put it on the floor and fifteen seconds later all the food was gone. Marmite gave it a final, hopeful lick then settled on his blanket in the corner, giving his paws a wash.

"The way he eats reminds me of the crew when they get back from a long shout. You take your life in your hands if you get in their way. I'm making stew for tonight."

"Can I help?" Jonty washed his hands and face to get rid of the dog slobber. "It needs to be something I can't damage too badly. I'm a hopeless cook."

"You can peel the potatoes," Steve said. "That's safe enough. Please don't chop off a finger."

Jonty settled at the table with a pile of potatoes and a bowl of water to put them in. He peeled steadily, glad of the mundane task to take his thoughts away from Jed's absence. He'd only known him a short while but he missed his solid, steady presence. *He's like an anchor, stopping me from drifting in aimless circles.*

"Penny for 'em?"

"Oh, sorry. I was daydreaming, wasn't I?"

"You were." Steve grinned. "Give me those spuds." He took the ones Jonty had finished. "Same amount again should do it."

Shrugging, Jonty carried on peeling.

"So what's it like to be an artist?" Steve asked.

Jonty had to think about how to answer. "I'm sure it's different for anyone who paints, but for me, it's possession. My entire body and mind taken over by the need to get color on canvas. To make the picture in my head come to life."

"Sounds intense."

"When I'm painting I don't notice how all-consuming it is. I prefer to be alone because I have a tendency to ignore anyone who tries to speak to me. My father thought I was a freak when I was younger. He threatened to send me to a military school." The usual pang of guilt swept through Jonty's body. He swallowed.

"It must be hard to talk about him. About your family." The fine lines around Steve's eyes crinkled in sympathy.

"Time makes it easier." Jonty sighed. "Survivor's guilt doesn't go away."

"Sorry. I didn't mean to be such a downer." Steve gave Jonty's shoulder a squeeze.

"You weren't. I've spent nearly a year hardly living and my family wouldn't want that—even my father. It's time to move on."

"And the auction will help you do that?"

"I think so." Jonty finished his last potato. "And I never said thank you to the lifeboat crew that saved me. I want to give something back."

"They don't want thanks. That's not why they do it."

"But they deserve it."

Steve threw a few chopped herbs into the massive stewpot. "This can go on now. It'll cook long and slow. You want to watch a movie or something?"

"Sure." Jonty accepted the need to change the subject with some relief. "So long as you don't mind me and Marm hanging around."

"Nah. I have to be here. Kennick will get on the radio when they're close to port, then I have to help with the landing. We can feed them before they head off home. It would be nice to have company."

It turned out to be a relaxing evening. Steve and Jonty watched comedies for a few hours with Marmite wedged between them on the sofa. He had his head on Jonty's lap, his tail on Steve's, and took up more room than the two of them combined. When the radio squawked into life, Jonty was dozing. He'd only had a few hours' sleep that morning and the lack of rest was catching up with him. He listened to Steve as he answered the call, then helped him open the boatshed doors, which wasn't an easy job on crutches. Twenty minutes later, the bright orange lifeboat appeared out of the darkness.

Jonty kept well out of the way while the boat was cranked up the launching ramp. He was a little anxious about Jed's reaction to finding him waiting, but excited at the same time. He needed confirmation that Jed had gotten home safe. While the crew got out of their gear, Jonty killed time by laying the table in the mess room and giving the stew a stir. It smelt delicious and Jonty hoped there might be enough for him to have a bowl too.

"Well, here's a welcome sight." Jed's gruff tones set Jonty's heart pounding.

"You're back!" He ran toward Jed, then froze. He wasn't sure how comfortable Jed might be with a public display of affection.

"Come here." Jed gathered Jonty into his arms, treating him to a bear hug that took his breath away. "Have you been good while I was away?"

Jonty managed a nod as the room filled with hungry lifeboat men and women. Jed introduced him to everyone and soon his head was spinning with all the names. He ended up at the table, a huge bowl of stew in front of him, with Jed on his right and Steve on his left.

"So this is your artist, Jed. Where have you been hiding him?"

Jonty remembered the speaker was Kennick Poldean, the coxswain. He leaned a bit closer to Jed.

"He's shy, Ken. You'll scare him." Jed put his arm around Jonty's shoulders.

"Pah. You've talked about him nonstop for the last six hours. Of course we're all curious to meet him. Jonty, this big lug usually manages a couple of sentences during a whole shout. Today I couldn't shut him up."

"Oh…I'm…I mean, I'm just me."

Kennick raised his bushy gray eyebrows and smiled. Jonty wanted to run away, as fast as possible. He focused on the stew, which was delicious, but only managed a few mouthfuls. He picked up pieces of conversation about the rescue of the injured sailor and resolved to ask Jed about it when they were alone. Soon, the meal was finished and people began to take their leave. Jed pushed his chair back.

"If Marmite can get his nose out of that bowl of leftover stew, I think it's time we made our way home."

Marmite gave his dish a last lick before ambling toward the door. Jonty giggled. "I think he agrees."

Jed said his goodbyes then tucked Jonty against his side. Jonty couldn't help but snuggle into his warmth as they walked outside into the chill night air.

"I'm so glad you were here waiting for me, Jonty." Jed gave him a squeeze. "Marmite's always pleased to see me, but it's not the same as having a person looking forward to my return.

"I had a good day. Steve helped look after Marmite. I think I made a friend. I like him."

"You made a lot of new friends today. The whole crew loved you."

Jonty didn't know what to say to that and they'd reached Jed's cottage. Marmite had already pushed his way inside, no doubt to claim his bed by the Aga.

"I should head home. It's been a really long day and…" He was silenced by a kiss.

"I don't think so, Jonathon Trelawn. You'll be keeping me warm in bed tonight."

"I will?" Jonty gulped.

"You will. But don't worry. Your virtue is safe because I'm exhausted." Jed stroked his hair. "Just to sleep, Jonty. Will you stay with me?"

Mute, Jonty nodded. He couldn't think of anything he wanted more.

"Don't think I've forgotten that you owe me a proper answer regarding our first date too."

That sent a shiver of need down Jonty's spine and, when he was certain Jed couldn't hear him, he whispered, "Yes, Sir."

Chapter Seven

Jed awoke feeling warmer than usual. He lay for a while, eyes closed, registering the weight across his chest. Jonty. When it came to bed occupation, Jonty was a space invader. He was even worse than Marmite, who was snoring on the floor at the side of the bed. Jonty seemed to be treating Jed like a giant teddy bear. He had slung a leg across Jed's thighs and the top half of his body was resting on Jed's chest, his head nestled beneath his chin. Jed cracked open an eye. A strand of blond hair tickled his ear. He would have been quite happy to be a Jonty mattress for the rest of the morning, but he needed the bathroom and when Marmite regained consciousness, he'd be wanting a walk. Jed tried to move without waking Jonty but it proved impossible.

"You're so comfy," Jonty murmured.

"And you're a serial snuggler." Jed stroked Jonty's hair. It was just as smooth and soft as he'd known it would be.

"Sorry." Jonty didn't move and didn't sound at all apologetic.

"Hmm, I don't think you are. I might have to punish you." Jed stroked a bare shoulder and waited for a reaction. Jonty wasn't quite awake and it took a while for Jed's words to sink in.

"I...what?" Jonty rolled off Jed's body in a flurry of tangled limbs. Jed had to catch him to prevent him falling out of bed completely. Marmite sat up, apparently curious at all the activity.

"I think you heard me." Jed chuckled and pulled Jonty back against him. "Naughty young men need to be corrected or they get out of hand."

Jonty's erection tented the bedcovers.

"What kind of punishment do you mean?" Jonty whispered. He slipped his hand beneath the bedcovers and Jed knew exactly where it was headed. He wasn't sure how far he should go. Jonty was an innocent in so many ways and Jed didn't want to scare him.

"Kneeling in a corner can be effective." Jed pretended to think. "For more serious infractions, a spanking sends a strong message."

Jonty whimpered. Beneath the bedclothes his hand was moving.

"Or, in extreme circumstances, I'm quite fond of chastity cages."

"Oh my God!" Naked, Jonty leapt from the bed and made a dash for the bathroom, dick in hand.

Laughing, Jed gave Marmite some ear scratches. "I don't think any of those suggestions turned him off, do you, Marm?" If it was possible for a dog to roll its eyes, that's what Marmite seemed to be doing. "Time to get up, boy. We'll let Jonty recover in his own time. It remains to be seen whether he'll come join us for breakfast or make a run for it." Jed really hoped for the former option. He pulled on an old pair of jeans and a thick sweater over a T-shirt then padded down the stairs, Marmite thumping along behind him. He used the small toilet next to the workshop to take care of essentials then set to creating a full English, a treat he reserved for weekends.

While he cooked, Jed thought back to the previous night. He'd been so happy to see Jonty at the lifeboat station. His shy smile of welcome had been the perfect tonic to a hard trip and the way he had glued himself to Jed's side during the noisy dinner — well, Jed loved to feel needed. Back home in the bedroom, Jonty had been so cute and bashful as he'd taken his clothes off, diving beneath the covers then peeking out while Jed stripped down to his underwear, watching every move. Jed had taken the quickest shower ever, not wanting to leave Jonty alone for any longer than necessary. Once he was under the duvet, eyes closing, Jed had held back a laugh as Jonty edged closer until skin touched skin. Jed had fallen asleep to the joyful sensation of Jonty's bare ass pressing back against his groin. Thank the Lord he'd been so tired or it would have been a frustrating night.

Of course he could have taken Jonty before he got up but teasing him was fun and Jed wanted him in the right frame of mind before they took the next step. Their relationship, friendship, was very new and Jed wasn't the type to take what he wanted then run. Jonty needed to be coaxed, encouraged — he'd soon be more able to express what he wanted and that had to come from him, not from Jed.

The man in Jed's thoughts appeared in the doorway. His hair was damp and pulled back from his face, which had a rosy glow.

"Take a seat. Breakfast is ready. I hope you're hungry."

Jonty chewed on his lower lip as if debating a decision, then pulled out a chair. "I'm starving."

Jed loaded two plates with fried potatoes, eggs, sausages, bacon, grilled tomatoes and mushrooms, baked beans and fried bread before joining Jonty at the table. "Eat up." Jed tucked into his own meal, not wanting to force conversation.

Jonty devoured every scrap of food. He licked his lips in a very provocative way then smacked them together in appreciation. "That was fantastic. I'm so full."

Jed cleared the table before pouring them both a mug of coffee. "I'll consider it my duty, and my pleasure, to keep you filled." He winked. "Milk?"

Jonty made a strangled sound halfway between a moan and a whimper. "That would be... That would be..."

"How about we take Marm for his morning constitutional? He needs to work off that bacon you slipped him and I think some fresh air might do us both good, don't you?"

"You saw that?"

"Yep."

"A walk sounds good." Jonty had guilt written all over him.

After finishing their coffee and doing a quick clear-up, they donned outdoor clothes and footwear before setting out.

Outside it was a beautiful, crisp morning. Sunshine glittered on the water and gulls screamed their greetings from the air. Marmite romped along the beach, dodging the waves, shoving his nose into rock pools to scare the hermit crabs. Jed kept an eye on him but his focus was on Jonty. He put an arm around his slender shoulders. "I hope I haven't scared you the last couple of days."

"Oh but you did," Jonty said. "When you went out on the lifeboat I was scared half to death. Steve calmed me down. He explained how much training you guys have and I managed not to worry too much."

"You know that's not what I meant, don't you?"

"Uh-huh, but that's the only time I got scared. Other times I was intrigued, excited…and really turned on."

It was Jed's turn to wonder if the heat in his cheeks was due to the breeze or a full-on blush.

"Are you a…a Dominant, Jed?"

"Straight to the point, eh?" Jed pulled Jonty a bit closer. "How much do you know about the BDSM lifestyle?"

"I went to art college in London. I'm not completely innocent. I had a couple of friends who played a bit and I've looked on the internet…but don't worry, I know that gay porn sites are not a realistic representation." Jonty giggled. "How they manage some of those positions is beyond me." He picked up a pebble, turning it over and over in his hand. "I kind of worked out that you might be a Dom. I don't think I'm going to like a lot of pain, Jed."

"I'm not a sadist, sweetheart. Well, not the kind that likes to inflict pain."

Jonty gave him a big-eyed stare. "So what kind are you?"

"Well, a submissive might consider orgasm control a form of sadism. Frustration can be agony, of a kind."

"You like to be in control, huh?"

Jed nodded. "In the bedroom, definitely. In other aspects of my life, I'm more flexible."

"Flexible how?"

"Well, if my partner wanted structure in their life, to hand over power for decision making, for example, I'm happy with that, but if they want to be more independent, that's good too. I used the word 'partner' deliberately, Jonty. I want a relationship, not an arrangement. I certainly don't want a slave or a man who feels obligated to drop to his knees every time I walk into a room." Some of Jonty's tension seemed to dissipate. "Do you think you're a submissive?"

"I think I *am* submissive. I don't know about *a* submissive. I don't know enough to say. I need to get some experience, I suppose." Jonty blinked, affecting innocence.

"Oh, there's definitely a brat under that sweet exterior, isn't there?" Jed was thrilled. Jonty wasn't jumping in feet first. He was demonstrating a sensible amount of caution without backing off completely. "So how about the question I asked you yesterday morning. Do you want to go out on a date with me?"

"Yes, Sir." Jonty made direct eye contact, his gaze unwavering.

"Then I will plan something special. It's Sunday tomorrow — do you have anything on?"

"Washing my hair," Jonty said with a cheeky grin. He started running away but didn't get far on the pebbles before Jed caught him, pulling them both down onto the beach. He cupped Jonty's face in his hands, leaning over him. Jonty parted his lips, all expectation. Jed couldn't disappoint him. The first contact between them was just a gentle tease. Jonty's lips were soft and he yielded to Jed's increased pressure. Jed grew more insistent, probing with his tongue until Jonty opened for him. He tasted sweet and warmth spread through Jed's body, despite the cold wind. Jonty moaned, kissing back with enthusiasm, and when he did pull away, Jed wanted to drag him back. Instead, he examined Jonty's stubble-burned cheeks and swollen lips.

"Perfect. Just perfect." Jonty should always look this way.

"We ought to get off the beach before we get arrested for public indecency," Jonty said.

"There's no one here but us." Jed took a deep breath. "But I should get back. I have work to catch up on after being out on the boat so long yesterday. I love being self-employed, but my weekends are often sacrificed to work."

"And I have so many ideas for new paintings!" Jonty exclaimed. "I want to get started."

"I wish I had better light at my place," Jed said. "There's plenty of room."

"I don't think I'd get much done if we were in the same space," Jonty said with a shy smile. "And I need to think about what to do with Cliff House. The light is the only good thing about that place. There are too many memories there. I need to move on and the house is part of what's holding me back. Spending time with you has given me more energy than I've had in months." Jonty bent to pick something up. "Pieces of sea glass are like jewels, aren't they?" He held up a smooth green pebble.

Jed chuckled. "Your mind flits around like a hummingbird sometimes." He whistled for Marmite, who shook a piece of seaweed from his nose before gamboling over to them. "Time to head home."

As they strolled back, Jonty was continually distracted by the treasure he found on the beach. Pretty shells, small crabs left by the receding tide, pebbles with seams of quartz. Jed caught the bug and found himself examining pieces of driftwood. "Perhaps I can find some wood to turn into a sculpture for your auction," he said.

"That would be so cool!" Jonty helped him look and even Marmite seemed to get with the program, though he tended to want sticks thrown for him rather than consider their artistic merits. The tideline was the best place to find bigger chunks of wood and Jed came across an intriguing branch worn smooth and silver by the water. He could see a shape in it and visualize how he might turn it into a piece of art.

"This one." He held it up.

"It's beautiful." Jonty stroked the wood.

Jed grabbed Jonty's hand. He kissed his palm, making him squirm and giggle. "I'll miss you today."

"Me too. I can't wait for our date. Where are we going?"

"It's a surprise. Just be ready at ten tomorrow morning. I'll come collect you." They walked along the quay toward Jed's cottage.

"Should I bring anything special?"

"Stop probing, Jonty. I'm not going to tell you anything more. And that pout, though adorable, is not going to get you anywhere."

Jonty stuck his lip out even further. "Will it get me a goodbye kiss?"

Jed placed his hand around the nape of Jonty's neck, beneath his hair. "Now that I can help you with."

Jonty's scent and taste were addictive. Jed knew he'd never be able to let him go.

* * * *

Jonty wandered from room to room at Cliff House, making a critical examination of the property. With a bit of love and effort it would make a fantastic family home and that's what it needed — a family. It needed kids' finger paintings on the walls, a kitten climbing the curtains and a Labrador getting hair on the couches. His mother had furnished the place using an interior designer and, though all the fixtures and fittings were high quality, they were a thousand miles away from Jonty's taste. There was also a huge garden, which he had little inclination to maintain. Jonty used one ensuite bedroom, his painting room and the kitchen. In all three he'd stripped out as many reminders of his family as he could. He had avoided putting the house on the market because it felt like a final betrayal of his family's memory. He had already sold the house in Surrey and the flat in London, his father's cars and his mother's collection of Regency furniture. It had all been handled for him by an agent, allowing him to remain detached from the process. The funds had been deposited in a savings account and he hadn't even glanced at a statement since.

The easy option would be to ring the same agent he'd used before and get them to arrange everything, but this time Jonty wanted to be more involved. He rang the only estate agent in the next village and arranged for someone to come for a valuation that evening, then he called Jed.

"This is Jed, what can I do for you?"

"Uh, hi, Jed...sorry to bother you..."

"Jonty? Are you okay? Is everything all right?" Jed's deep tones and his concern sent a ripple of arousal down Jonty's spine.

"Oh yes, really. I'm fine." *Missing you.* "But I wondered if I could ask a favor?"

"Whatever you need." Jed sounded so certain, it made Jonty smile.

"I have an appointment with an estate agent this evening—he's coming round to value the house. Do you think you could be here with me? He's coming at seven."

"I'll be there at six-thirty." Without saying it, Jed's tone implied that any other scenario was not an option. "Who did you call?"

"Bateman's," Jonty replied. "Is that okay?"

"Sure. I know Freddie Bateman and his dad. I made all the shelving units and the desks for their office. They won't rip you off."

"And you're sure you're not too busy?" Jonty nipped his lower lip.

"I've been here, working away, wondering how I was going to sleep without you in my bed tonight."

"Oh..." Jonty didn't know how to respond. He'd been thinking the exact same thing.

"You'll come home with me once we're done with the estate agent."

"I will?"

"You will. See you later, Jonty."

Jonty disconnected the call. He couldn't help but grin. *Maybe tonight he'll... Oh wow! I need to shower and...stuff.* He rubbed his belly. Enemas were not something he enjoyed but they were worth it for the fun that followed. He checked his watch, realizing he still had a few hours to paint. There was nothing to clean up in the house. He wasn't a neat freak but he didn't make much mess other than in his painting room and there wasn't much he could do about color-splattered floorboards.

With a fresh canvas on his easel, Jonty flipped through his sketchbook, deciding which image to use for the first picture in the series he planned. He mixed a thin gray watercolor to make some rough outlines then got started.

The next thing he knew there was a banging at the front door. He had no idea how long whoever his visitor was had been knocking. Still grasping his brush, he went to the door, which he pulled open.

"Jed! I wasn't expecting you until later."

"It is later." Jed pulled him in for a hug before treating him to a blood-heating kiss.

"What do you mean?" Jonty asked when he got his breath back.

"It's six-thirty, Jonty. You've been painting, haven't you?"

"I…yes, but it can't have been that long… I need to shower and…"

"Hey. Calm down." Jed ushered him into the hall. "There's no rush. Go take your time in the bathroom. I'll make a pot of coffee and keep an ear out for Freddie." When he smiled, the fine lines around Jed's eyes crinkled and he got a slight dimple in one cheek. He made Jonty melt inside. Jonty thrust his paintbrush into Jed's hand then tore up the stairs. Perhaps if he jacked off in the shower, he might be able to think straight.

Once he was naked and standing beneath the hot shower spray, Jonty didn't find clarity. Instead, the steam seemed to be fogging his mind as well as the shower screen. Idly, he drew a heart on the glass with his finger. His balls ached and his dick was stiff but all he could think about was Jed's low voice talking about orgasm control. *Jed didn't say I could touch myself.* Jonty sighed. *He didn't say you couldn't either, idiot.* A hand strayed toward his erection, moving of its own volition. Jonty distracted himself by turning the temperature down. He squeaked as the water turned frigid. *What am I doing? We haven't even slept together yet…though that can't happen soon enough for me.* He grinned and finished washing, stiff dick forgotten. He took his time with the enema, mumbling and cursing the whole time. *He's worth it. Soooo worth it.* With the whole uncomfortable process over, Jonty sat for a while on the toilet, head in his hands, taking deep breaths. He wondered what it would be like to have Jed help him out. He could do with someone rubbing his back and whispering soothing words in his ear.

Squeaky clean inside and out, Jonty dressed in jeans that were tighter than the pairs he normally wore. He dug in the back of a drawer until he found a fine-knit cashmere sweater that was the exact same blue as Jed's eyes. The fabric was so soft against his skin, it felt like a hug. It had been a Christmas gift from his mother and for a moment, Jonty could almost feel her arms around him. He snuffled, but for once his memories didn't darken his mood. Instead he was able to remember a good time instead of tragedy. He decided footwear might be an idea if he had to walk all over the house, so he donned socks and a pair of plain black trainers. He gave his hair an extra rub with a towel before yanking it back into a loose ponytail. He'd worry about drying it properly once the estate agent was gone.

There were voices coming from the kitchen when Jonty trotted down the stairs. He found Jed handing a mug of something to a man he assumed was Freddie Bateman.

"Oh, hey, Jonty. I made fresh coffee, you want one?" Jed waved a mug in his direction.

"Yes, please." Jonty moved to Jed's side, immediately feeling more secure about meeting someone new. Jed handed him a drink and for a moment their fingers touched. The contact and Jed's reassuring smile were all Jonty needed.

"Hi, I'm Jonty Trelawn." He gave Freddie Bateman a quick once-over. Smart suit, broad shoulders, clean-shaven. He had dark brown hair, hazel eyes and a wide smile.

"It's a pleasure to meet you, Mr. Trelawn. This is a great place you have here."

"Please call me Jonty."

"Sure. How about I take a look around? If I have any questions, I'll come back here with them."

"Oh, yes…that would be great." Jonty tried not to sound too relieved that he didn't have to visit every room again. He leaned against the kitchen counter, cradling his mug, not meeting Jed's eyes.

"It's tough, isn't it?" Jed came to lean next to him. "Letting go of the past. I'm proud of you."

"Harder than I thought." Jonty sighed. "Am I doing the right thing, Jed?" He leaned against Jed's side, absorbing his warmth.

"Only you can answer that. I can tell you that Freddie is delighted to get this listing. He has a queue of people waiting for bigger properties around here. It will likely sell fast."

"I need to find a place for me too."

"I have an idea about that. You know the lighthouse out on the headland?"

"Sure, it's been abandoned for years." Jonty could picture the white structure with its light at the top.

"It's up for sale. There are living quarters on two floors and the room at the top would make an amazing space for you to paint now that all the light fittings have been taken out." He put his arm around Jonty's shoulders. "Of course, it would need some work."

"It sounds perfect!"

"Freddie has it on his books. Hasn't even had a sniff of interest because there's only one bedroom and there's a clause written into the deeds that it can't be used as a holiday let."

"Can we go take a look?" Jonty bounced on his toes until Jed pulled him closer.

"Down, boy. It's dark now and I have other plans for you this evening."

Jonty gulped. "That sounds…nice." He wished he'd given himself some relief in the shower because his jeans were far too tight to be comfortable when housing an erection. He wiggled, trying to get comfortable. Jed spun him around until they were face to face and so close that Jonty's hard dick pressed against Jed's hip. Jed pushed Jonty's arms behind his back then held them there, encircling his wrists with one large hand. Jonty stilled. A sense of peace enveloped him and when Jed leaned down for a kiss, his world was complete.

A discreet cough from the kitchen door broke the spell. Jonty buried his head against Jed's chest, not wanting to move.

"All done, Freddie?" Jed asked.

"I'll need to come back to look at the grounds in the light, but I'll write all this up and give Jonty a call to get everything cleared."

Jonty lifted his head and gave Jed an appealing look.

"You can call me, Freddie. Jonty will be with me."

"Sure. Have a good evening, guys. I'll let myself out." Freddie chuckled all the way to the door.

"Those eyes of yours should be registered as lethal weapons," Jed murmured. "Spaniel puppies have nothing on you."

"Talking of dogs," Jonty said, "where's Marmite?"

"I couldn't persuade him to move his lazy behind away from the Aga. Uphill isn't Marm's favorite direction."

Jonty giggled, rubbing his face against the hard planes of Jed's chest. "Then we should go make sure he's okay, shouldn't we?"

"Pack a toothbrush. You won't be needing clothes."

Jonty pelted up the stairs to grab an overnight bag. Within ten minutes he and Jed were strolling down the hill toward the bay. Jonty would have skipped if it hadn't been for Jed holding him close to his side.

"Thank you for coming this evening. Everything seems so much easier to handle when you're there with me," Jonty said.

"You did fine." Jed lengthened his pace, apparently in a hurry. "And there's nothing wrong with wanting support. I'm happy to be there for you whenever you need me."

"Need you now," Jonty whispered. "Deep inside me."

"I have great hearing, Jonty. Did you know that?" They reached the cottage door, which Jed kicked open.

He slung Jonty over his shoulder before hauling him up the stairs.

"Ooh, caveman. I like it!" No drug could have induced Jonty's high. He dropped the bag he was still clutching, watching it bounce down the stairs. He lost his sense of perspective for a moment as the world turned, then he landed on Jed's mattress with a bounce. An instant later, Jed straddled him.

"I had every intention of taking this slow." He pushed a strand of hair away from Jonty's eyes. "But *you* are temptation walking and I think you know full well what you do to me."

Jonty tried for an innocent expression. It didn't work. Jed's knees pressed into his hips, keeping him in place.

"Keep still." Jed's low growl went straight to Jonty's dick. When Jed began to undo Jonty's belt buckle, Jonty thought he might come there and then. He took short, deep breaths. "You need a brown paper bag?" Jed asked.

"If you keep touching me, I'm going to come," Jonty pleaded.

"Not gonna happen. Not till I say so." Jed slid the belt free then used it to strap Jonty's wrists to the brass bedstead. Jonty tugged on the bonds but they held, the leather digging into his skin. The sensation thrilled him to his core. He realized that the whimpering sounds he could hear were coming from his own mouth as Jed did an efficient job of ridding him of his shoes, socks and jeans. He shoved Jonty's shirt up around his neck, baring his chest.

"What a pretty picture." Jed took a firm grasp of Jonty's cock, making him cry out. "This is mine now. Your pleasure, your release — they belong to me."

"Yes, Sir!"

"We need to talk about a safe word. You know what that is?"

"Uh-huh."

"It should be something you remember but that you wouldn't normally use…like sea cow."

"Sea cow?" Jonty couldn't stop laughing. "Where did that come from?"

"It's just an example." Jed shook his head. "It popped into my mind."

"How about starfish? I'm less likely to get hysterical if I have to use it."

"Perfect. Stay put."

Jonty giggled. He couldn't move anyway. "Why would I want to go anywhere?" He bent his knees, tilting his hips. His rigid cock swayed.

"I knew all along you were a brat."

"What are you doing?" Jonty strained to see what Jed was up to. A sudden constriction around the base of his balls gave him a clue.

"Your dick looks even prettier with a cock ring around it."

"It squeezes!"

"It's supposed to. It's going to stop you from coming before I want you to." Jed gave the tip of Jonty's cock a kiss, making him squeal.

"But *I* want to…" Jonty lost the power of speech as Jed swallowed him to the root. He was reduced to incoherent babbling as Jed sucked him hard. When Jed finally pulled away, Jonty didn't know whether to laugh, scream or cry. "Don't stop!" he wailed.

"My dick. My balls. My arse." Jed lifted Jonty's legs and gave his backside a firm smack. "You can't have forgotten that already."

"You're an evil, evil man..." Warmth spread across Jonty's butt and he hoped Jed might spank him again. Instead he was rewarded with the glorious sight of Jed removing his shirt. Jonty didn't care if he was drooling — Jed was worth it. When his jeans followed, all the moisture in Jonty's mouth evaporated. Jed's briefs were in a very intimate relationship with his skin. *Is it appropriate to be jealous of underwear?* Jonty wondered. Then Jed shucked off the scrap of fabric and Jonty's world ceased to turn.

"Oh my..." Any more words Jonty might have managed were stifled by a kiss. A long, thorough, exceptional kiss. When he was done, Jed stood back and for a while just smiled. "Jed...I'm dying here. I need you. Please don't make me beg." Jonty would happily get on his knees and kiss Jed's feet if it meant he'd be rewarded with that long, thick masterpiece filling his arse. Only he couldn't, because he was tied to the damn bed.

"Patience, gorgeous. Good things come to he who waits." Jed put all the emphasis on the word 'come'.

"Evil." Jonty didn't want to wait. He wanted Jed inside him but Jed had different ideas. He proceeded to stroke, lick and bite every inch of Jonty's body. He sucked up marks on every erogenous zone Jonty possessed and a few he hadn't known about, leaving him incoherent with need. He knew the instant Jed moved away. "No! Don't go..."

"It's okay, gorgeous. Not going anywhere except to fetch supplies." Jed sounded far away even though he was only on the other side of the room.

"Thank God!" If being a submissive meant being frustrated to the point of pain, Jonty was considering switching to the dominant side of the fence.

"Of course, I could make you wait a bit longer." Jed flicked the tip of Jonty's cock, making him arch off the bed. "Tease you a while. Bring you to the edge over and over until you scream. Would you like that, Jonty?"

"No! I mean…whatever you want, Sir. Oh God, no, that's a lie. Please, please fuck me, Jed. Now!" He was answered by the press of a slick finger against his hole.

"It's been a while for you, hasn't it?" Jed asked.

Jonty had no idea how Jed expected him to be able to come up with sensible responses. He wriggled, trying to persuade Jed's finger deeper.

"Relax and let me in."

Jed's soothing tones seeped into Jonty's chaotic thoughts. He made a conscious effort to relax and was rewarded by a touch inside him that sent shooting stars across his vision. "Ohhhh!" His wail was loud enough to let the entire village know what he and Jed were up to. He clamped his lips together.

"The walls here are two feet thick, Jonty. No one can hear you scream." Jed used a fake evil villain voice, sending Jonty into peals of laughter. "Or I could introduce you to my gag collection."

"You have a collection?" Jonty squirmed, desperate to be filled.

"Uh-huh."

The rip of foil told Jonty things might finally be moving in the direction he needed. Jed hoisted one of Jonty's legs onto his shoulder. When he pressed his gloved cock against Jonty's fluttering hole, Jonty howled his relief.

"Yes! In me. Now, now, now!"

Jed pushed forward so just his tip entered Jonty's channel. "Who's in charge here, brat?"

"Damn it!" Jonty cursed the belt around his wrists, Jed's glacial pace and the world in general. "You are, Sir."

"Right answer." Jed thrust forward, making Jonty's head spin. From one finger to Jed's ample girth was quite a leap. The burn made Jonty's eyes water but the initial pain soon faded, allowing him to absorb the delicious sensation of being utterly filled. When Jed began to move, slowly at first, then with more force, liquid fire filled Jonty's veins. He needed to come with a desperation bordering on panic but couldn't vocalize his need. Not that it would make any difference. Jed was implacable in his control. He'd move at his pace and no other—Jonty didn't dare complain in case Jed slowed down or pulled away just to punish him.

"You feel perfect." Jed grabbed Jonty's other leg, resting his calf on one shoulder, then pressed forward, bending Jonty double. The position served to deepen his penetration and Jonty yelled his approval. Jed began to thrust in earnest, his face a study in focused concentration. Jonty tingled from the tips of his toes to the hairs on his head, his orgasm held at bay only by the restrictive ring around his cock. Then Jed reached between them, flicked the ring free then took Jonty's aching shaft into his fist. He jacked Jonty's cock in time with forceful thrusts and there was no way in Heaven or on Earth that Jonty could stop himself from coming. He spurted again and again into Jed's hand, helpless to resist as Jed milked him dry. Then Jed grabbed Jonty's hips and hammered home his claim, yelling Jonty's name as he came.

After a few delicious moments of cum-scented air, heavy breathing and sticky skin, Jed pulled out, lowering Jonty's trembling legs to the bed. He unfastened Jonty's wrists then pulled Jonty onto his chest, hugging him tight.

"That was perfect. You were perfect, Jonty."

Jonty lost his breath to a kiss. His wrists ached. His arse ached more. He loved every twinge. He fell asleep clinging to Jed's chest.

Chapter Eight

"Do you know how long it's been since I went on an actual date?" Jonty, standing in Jed's kitchen, vibrated with excitement. "Never. I've never been on a proper date. Where are we going?"

"As I've already told you, several times, it's a surprise." Jed put the last of the breakfast dishes away. He loved how excited Jonty was about their date and hoped the day wouldn't be a disappointment. A tap at the door brought Marmite to his feet, ears pricked and tail wagging. "Not much of a guard dog, are you, Marm?" Jed gave him an affectionate pat as he passed.

"Come on in, Beth." The door opened and Beth Arnold, lugging a huge picnic basket, struggled inside. Jed relieved her of the basket, setting it on the table.

"Thought I'd save you a trip to The Crab to pick this up, Jed. Oh, you must be Jonty." She pulled Jonty into a hug, much to Jed's amusement.

"Um, hello?" Jonty seemed a bit shell-shocked.

"Jonty, this is Beth from The Crusty Crab. She does some catering as a side line and I ordered us a picnic for today."

"Wow! Can I see…?" Jonty poked at the basket but Jed pushed his hand away.

"You're worse than Marmite. No peeking."

Jonty pouted and Beth chuckled. "You two boys have a great day. I hope we'll see you both in The Crab soon. Don't do anything I wouldn't do."

"That doesn't leave much," Jed said, as he escorted her out.

"Cheeky boy." Beth ruffled his hair. "Have fun. It's about time you did."

Jed returned to the kitchen with warm cheeks. "Sorry about that. She mothers me."

"I like her!" Jonty grinned. "And she brought food. You've gone to so much trouble. I'm impressed."

"We'll see. Why don't you get your shoes on and fetch a coat. It's cold and we have a way to walk."

While Jonty was getting ready to leave, Jed made last-minute preparations, stowing a few things into a backpack. His thoughts drifted back to waking next to Jonty that morning, something he hoped he'd be doing every day from now on. Jonty seemed so much more relaxed in sleep with all the worry lines smoothed from his face. Jed had woken him with a kiss, nothing more. He wanted Jonty needy by the time they reached their destination and that meant no morning blow jobs and no exploring the man's tempting arse.

Jonty bounded into the kitchen. "I'm ready!"

"Not quite."

Jonty gave him a quizzical look.

"Drop your trousers and bend over the table."

"What?"

"You heard me." Jed softened his words with what he hoped was a reassuring smile.

"I... Okay." Jonty lowered his zipper then shimmied his hips until his jeans fell to his knees. He had on a tiny red thong, which nestled between his butt cheeks. Jed remained implacable when he hesitated. One raised eyebrow was all it took for Jonty to roll the scrap of fabric over his hips.

"Spread your legs as far as you can," Jed ordered.

Jonty shuffled his feet apart before bending over the table. *Christ, what a beautiful picture he makes.* Jed gave Jonty's backside a pat. "I have a treat for you. Keep nice and still." He retrieved the toy and lube he'd stashed in a drawer.

"What are you doing?" Jonty asked, peering over his shoulder.

Jed lubed the smooth, egg-shaped vibrator then pressed it against Jonty's hole. "Just providing a bit of extra entertainment for our date."

"It's cold!"

"It will soon warm up. Let it in, Jonty." Jonty's muscles relaxed so Jed could push the toy inside him. When he was content it was properly seated, Jed pulled Jonty's underwear and jeans back into place. He felt in his pocket for the small remote control unit and, as Jonty was fastening his jeans, Jed switched it on.

"Oh, oh, oh!" Jonty danced around the kitchen. Marmite gave him a head-butt to the thigh as he passed. "What did you do?"

"Let's go. I'm sure a brisk walk will calm you down." Jed hoisted the backpack onto his shoulder then picked up the picnic basket. The toy had an eight-hour battery life before it needed recharging — plenty of time to ensure Jonty had a stimulating day.

The weather was perfect for walking. It was one of those clear days that had an invigorating snap in the air but enough warmth in the sun that it didn't matter. Jonty cast frequent baleful glares at Jed, which Jed pretended not to notice. Marmite bounded ahead of them sniffing at every lamppost, pillar and wall. They passed some other dog walkers with a pair of corgis and paused while Marmite allowed the two smaller dogs to greet him with appropriate deference. There were quite a few people out and about enjoying their Sunday, walking on the beach or sitting on the quay with crab buckets and lines. Jed noticed the smiles and knowing glances sent their way. He and Jonty would no doubt be the talk of The Crusty Crab by lunchtime. That was okay by him. He had no problem with people knowing that Jonty was his — in fact, he preferred it that way. There weren't that many gay men in the area but news traveled fast in small communities and Jonty was fresh to the scene. That made him a target. Jed tried not to think about his competition and focused on the walk instead. Watching Jonty squirm was huge fun and he had no intention of switching the vibrator off just yet. Hiking definitely had to be part of their future.

Jonty half walked, half skipped along the quay and Jed wasn't sure if that was because of his excitement for their date or because of the toy lodged firmly in his ass. He was tempted to turn the vibration level up, but resisted. Jonty was brand new to having his pleasure controlled by another man — he needed time to get used to all the new sensations Jed was introducing him to.

"Will you tell me where we're going now?" Jonty asked.

"You'll be able to guess in a minute anyway," Jed replied. They walked along the curve of the bay toward the headland, then followed the marked cliff path, which sloped upward from the beach. At this point on the coastline the cliffs weren't too high but the walk was still enough to get Jed's muscles working. As they rounded a curve at the top of the slope, their destination came into view. The lighthouse was a stubby white building rather than a majestic red and white striped beacon. It still had the glass top but the huge bulbs had long since been removed. The etched panes glistened in the sunlight.

Jonty gave a whoop of joy. "Please tell me we're going to the lighthouse." He bounced on the spot, as excited as a puppy on his first walk.

"We are. Not the most glamorous of locations for a first date, but I thought you might like to see it."

"It's perfect!" Jonty exclaimed. "I can't think of anywhere I'd rather go. Ever since you mentioned it yesterday I've been dying to take a look because it sounds perfect for a studio."

"Don't build your hopes up too much. It needs quite a lot of work and you might think that the light isn't right or something." Despite his words, Jed had a sense of deep contentment. Making Jonty happy made him happy.

It took them another ten minutes to reach the base of the lighthouse. Jed handed Jonty the key, which was an old-fashioned iron relic. "Here you go. You should do the honors."

Jonty inserted the key into the lock then twisted. There was a rough grating sound but the key turned with a little effort. The door opened with an un-oiled creak.

"Wow!" Jonty declared. "It sounds like a haunted house. I wonder if there are any ghosts here."

"Probably," Jed replied. "It wouldn't surprise me if the spirit of some old lighthouse keeper kept an eye on the place. You'll just have to behave, won't you?"

"But I thought making me behave was your job." Jonty batted his lashes.

Jed turned the remote up a notch.

"Hey! Stop that. You're making it hard to move."

"Oh, I'm glad I'm making it hard." Jed reduced the vibration back to a low buzz. "Should have put you in a cock cage too. Shame I forgot to pack one."

Jonty gulped. "Not helping. Not helping at all."

Jed chuckled. "This place isn't nearly as bad as I thought it was going to be. It wouldn't take much to clean it up. From the details Freddie Bateman gave me, there's this room, which is a lounge-cum-kitchen with two large storage lockers. Upstairs there's a bedroom and small bathroom. There's an oil-fired generator out back and a cesspit for sewerage, so it's basic but livable."

"Can we go up to the next floor?" Jonty asked. "I love the spiral staircase."

"Sure." Jed followed as Jonty and Marmite scampered up the stairs. They opened into a large, well-lit space with several windows. A bed frame stood in one corner, along with a dusty oak chest. Through a small door Jed could see a tiny bathroom.

"This is great!" Jonty exclaimed. "It would make a perfect gallery space. Do you think anyone would bother to walk out here to visit?"

"I'm sure they would." Jed dumped the picnic basket and rucksack on the floor. "I'd bet they couldn't get that bed frame down the stairs. How in the hell it got up here is a mystery." He took a folding water bowl from the rucksack, filled it from a bottle of water then put it on the floor for Marmite.

"A few planks on the base and it would make a perfect display area for sculptures." Jonty ran up the next set of stairs. "It's the light room!" His voice echoed from the room above.

Jed smiled at Jonty's excitement. He left Marmite slopping water over the floor and when he reached the top floor, he found Jonty with his hands pressed to the glass, staring at the view. "The horizon's always there. I think that's a line from a song...or maybe a poem. I can't recall."

"The trick is to make sure your anchor is well set." Jed moved behind Jonty who immediately leaned back against him. He put his arms around Jonty's waist, pulling him closer.

"When I lost my family, people thought I was mad to move down here where the sea would be a constant reminder of what happened, and perhaps there was an element of survivor's guilt. I didn't come here to torture myself, though. London, the house in Surrey, they were so confined. I felt like I was in prison. I couldn't breathe. When I got here, at first I couldn't bear to look at the sea. It took my family." Jonty took a deep, shuddering breath. "But, over time, I felt a connection, as if their spirits are carried by the waves."

A few strands of hair had escaped their tie. Jed pushed them to one side then kissed Jonty's neck. "The sea is a powerful entity. It's a reminder of just how small we are in the scheme of things. I think that's why a lot of the people who live here are realists — they understand their place in the world."

"That's what I want," Jonty murmured. "I need to know what I am. An artist, an orphan, a...submissive."

"A survivor. A strong, creative spirit with a gentle soul." Jed freed the rest of Jonty's hair. "*My* submissive."

"Am I?" Jonty turned in Jed's arms.

"If there's one thing I'm certain of, it's that." Jed switched off the remote in his pocket. "I want you to strip for me, Jonty."

Jonty blushed. He peeked at Jed from beneath his lashes, nibbling on his lower lip. Jed didn't say anything. He took a single pace back to give Jonty room to move. Room to obey.

Jonty bared his skin piece by enticing piece until he stood naked for Jed's appreciation.

"Are you cold?" The room was warmed by the sun through the glass but Jed didn't want Jonty uncomfortable.

"No, Sir."

"Good. Turn around. Put your hands on the glass at shoulder height." Once Jonty was in the position Jed wanted, he pulled lube and a condom from the backpack. There was also a thick blanket, which he laid on the floor for Jonty to stand on. He stripped off his top but left his jeans and footwear on. After unzipping, he sheathed his aching cock then slathered it and two fingers in lube. It may have been Jonty with a toy up his arse but Jed felt every vibration he'd created as a tingle in his balls. He'd been hard since they'd left home. "Look at the sea, Jonty. What's out there doesn't matter. What matters is you and me in this moment." He extracted the toy before probing Jonty's channel with two lubed fingers, encouraging the muscles to relax with gentle strokes. "Spread your legs a little wider." He fucked Jonty with his fingers until Jonty's breathing came in rapid pants. Their height difference made it difficult to take Jonty standing but Jed had a better idea. He got between Jonty and the window then picked him up. "Wrap your legs around me." With Jonty's arms around his neck and his legs around his waist, Jed had his burden secure. Jonty hardly weighed anything, it seemed. It took a bit of maneuvering but with the lube inside Jonty and the coating on Jed's dick, he slipped easily into Jonty's channel. Jed rested his shoulders on the glass for more stability. Jonty's heels dug into the top of his arse and he whimpered.

"Jed, please move. I..."

Jed set a rhythm of lifting Jonty a little then letting him slide down his cock. He did it over and over, speeding up then slowing down. Jonty's erection pressed against Jed's belly, leaving liquid silver trails. "Time for you to do some of the work, sweetheart." Holding Jonty tight to him, Jed lowered himself to the blanket. He rocked back until he was flat, with Jonty straddling him, still firmly impaled. "Ride me. But you don't get to come until I say you can." Jed put steadying hands on Jonty's hips, keeping him exactly where he wanted him. Jonty's entire body undulated as he rose and fell, muscles rippling. His cock bobbed. Jed relaxed and allowed the sensations to roll over him, his orgasm building with inexorable intent. Jonty threw his head back, his lips parted in a silent scream. A fine sheen of perspiration coated his chest and his nipples were hard peaks. Jed pictured how they might be improved with a pair of clamps joined by a chain that he could tug. He reached up and tweaked one pink nub, pinching and twisting. Jonty gasped and moved faster.

"Jed! Sir. I can't... I'm going to..."

"You can let it happen, Jonty." Jed took control, raising his knees to give Jonty support while he lifted him enough that Jed's erection almost came free of Jonty's grasping channel, then he tensed his stomach muscles and allowed Jonty to fall. Jonty made a grab for his cock. He came from a single touch and the warmth of his cum splattering Jed's chest set Jed off too. With a roar of release, he filled the condom.

Jonty collapsed onto Jed's chest, taking deep, heaving breaths. Jed's softening cock was still lodged inside him and he wished he could stay that way, but it wasn't practical, or comfortable. He eased free then settled Jonty to one side so he could remove the condom. Jonty snuggled against him as if magnetic attraction didn't allow him to get further away. A blanket on a concrete floor wasn't the most luxurious resting place, but Jed would lie on broken glass if it meant keeping Jonty close.

"That was…amazing," Jonty whispered. "Can we do it again?" He nuzzled beneath Jed's chin.

"Not just yet." Jed chuckled. "My powers of recuperation are good…they're not miraculous."

"You're so strong—staring at that view while you had me in your arms, while you were in me—do you think we traumatized the seagulls?"

"The places your mind wanders amaze me." Jed kissed the top of Jonty's head. Jonty shivered. "You're getting cold. Time to clean up and get dressed." Jed reached for the pack and the packet of wipes he'd stashed there.

"How come we've ended up with me naked and you still partly dressed?" Jonty squeaked as Jed dabbed at him with a wipe. "Not that I'm complaining."

"Because that's the way I like you—butt naked and at my mercy."

"Here, let me…" Jonty grabbed a wipe then set to cleaning Jed's chest. "Love your fur."

"I don't have that much." Jed peered at the scattering of dark hair across his chest.

"More than me. I don't have a single, solitary hair."

"And I like you that way, so we make a great pair. In fact…" Jed pushed his fingers toward Jonty's groin. "I think these should go too."

"You want me to shave…down there!" Jonty's indignant tone made Jed laugh.

"No. I'll do it for you." Seated across Jed's thighs, Jonty covered his dick. Jed moved his hands away. "No covering up. That's mine, remember?"

"I love it when you get all possessive." Jonty's dick began to harden.

"I can see that." Jed grinned. "But it's time to eat. Put your T-shirt and sweater on." When Jonty scrambled off his lap, Jed missed the weight. He had an irrational urge to keep Jonty as close as possible. He distracted himself by zipping up then retrieving his top layers. "Leave your trousers off, Jonty."

"Huh?" Jonty had underwear dangling from his finger.

"Nothing on your bottom half."

"Oh!" Jonty's erection stiffened.

Jed positioned himself with his back to a window, pulling the picnic basket to his side. "Now, let's see what's for lunch, shall we?" He opened the lid. "Crab sandwiches of course." He lifted packets wrapped in foil from the basket, leaving them within easy reach.

"Um, Jed?" Jonty's plaintive tone made Jed smile.

"Touch yourself. You don't have permission to come. Pickled eggs. Excellent."

Jonty sat cross-legged. He took a loose hold of his cock, stroking slowly, frowning in concentration. Marmite's dark head appeared in the stairwell. He bounded over to Jed.

"Typical. Just the sniff of food and you appear." Jed ruffled his ears.

"Jed! I can't keep doing this in front of Marmite. He's...young and impressionable."

"He's hungry. As usual. You stop when I tell you to and not before." Jed extracted a dog chew from the rucksack. He gave it to Marmite who took it to the opposite side of the room where he settled down for a good gnaw.

"But I..."

"Do you want to be punished, Jonty?" The flush on Jonty's cheeks told Jed he wasn't averse to the idea even though he shook his head. "Then bring yourself to the edge. I want you so close to orgasm you think it's unstoppable."

Jonty moved his hand faster, whimpering his frustration.

"Stop." Jed snapped out the word.

Jonty froze. "No! Jed, please..."

Jed pulled Jonty into his lap, Jonty's back against his chest. He kissed his neck and at the same time reached around him to grip his cock. Jonty's shaft was burning hot in Jed's hand. He stroked once from tip to root then cradled Jonty's balls. "Come."

Jonty arched his back, muscles straining. Jets of cum coated Jed's hand.

"Oh God, oh God, oh God!" Jonty's bare feet scrabbled for purchase on the rug.

"I've got you, sweetheart. Just let go." Jed held Jonty tight as he shook through the aftershock of orgasm. His release was more than just physical. He had allowed Jed to control him, given him the gift of trust. Tears welled in Jed's eyes but didn't fall. Deep satisfaction enveloped him and he stroked Jonty's flank until he calmed. They sat in silence for a few minutes, the only sound Marmite crunching his treat.

"Marmite's making me hungry, Jed. Can I have a sandwich now?"

"I think you've earned one." Jed cleaned his hands then Jonty's softened dick. "You can dress. Leaving you bare is too much temptation."

Jonty rolled onto his stomach then put his chin in his hands, giving Jed a perfect view of the smooth mounds of his arse. "Tempting? Me? I don't know what you mean."

Shaking his head, Jed started to unwrap parcels of food. "Eat, Jonty, before I decide to put your mouth to better use."

Jonty didn't respond. He fluttered his lashes, licked his lips and reached for a sandwich.

Chapter Nine

Over the next few weeks, Jonty couldn't recall ever being happier, even before the horror of losing his family. He had jumped at the chance to buy the lighthouse and the deal progressed quickly. He had great fun planning all the changes he wanted to make. He had commissioned Jed to make bespoke display units and shelving for the gallery area, agreeing to a price that Jonty knew was too low but Jed wouldn't budge on. Cliff House had sold to a local family with four children, with Jed instrumental in agreeing a deal they could afford. It hadn't even gone on the market so Jonty hadn't had to worry about showing people around. He'd already moved out everything he needed and just went back there to paint, something that he was doing more and more. His nights were spent at Jed's place. He was becoming known around the village as he sat on the quay sketching and, though still shy about talking to people, he no longer ran away when they approached. He'd also started volunteering at the lifeboat station and was painting a set of watercolors, featuring the boat and crew, to turn into new postcards for the kiosk there.

With three weeks to go before the auction, he had yet to finish his own offering, hence his current position with a sketchpad on his knees observing the lifeboat crew as they trained. Of course he wasn't getting a lot done because Jed in his RNLI uniform was far too distracting.

Jonty gave Marmite a scratch behind the ears. "He'll be done soon, boy. I promise." At his feet, Marmite rolled onto his back, demanding a belly rub. Jonty got to his knees to oblige, digging his fingers into Marmite's soft fur. "You are such an attention seeker," Jonty murmured.

"It's taken you a while to work that one out, and I have to say, you look spectacular on your knees."

"Jed!" Jonty scrambled to his feet. "Are you all finished?"

"We are. How did your sketching go? Can I see?"

Jonty bit his lip but handed over his pad. Jed flicked through the pages, his grin widening. "You seem to be obsessed with one particular subject."

"Well, it's especially inspiring." Jonty's cheeks heated. Every sketch he'd done was of Jed. The man did have a body worthy of art after all. "They'd be even better if you were naked," he whispered.

"It sounds to me like someone needs my personal attention. Time to go home."

Jonty gathered his things, shoving pencils and paper into his satchel as quickly as he could. Marmite caught the mood and headed for home at a rapid trot.

"I *would* like to draw you some time if you'd let me…I mean, you know…"

"Without my clothes on." Jed gave him the kind of smile that made Jonty's knees shake. He nodded his head so fast his vision blurred. "Okay."

"Did you just say I could…?"

"Sure. Why not? It could be fun, especially if you draw naked and I put you in chastity first."

Jonty gulped. "That would be so cruel!"

"No, it would enhance your concentration." They reached the cottage door and Marmite nosed his way inside. "And I'd enjoy it a lot."

Jonty was so hard it hurt. They hadn't tried chastity play yet but it was something that made him all hot and shivery when he thought about it.

"You know, you can get a setup that's a belt with a chastity device and a butt plug all in one. You'd look really good in one of those."

"I don't think I would!" Jonty shifted his weight from one foot to the other.

"We'll take a look online later and pick something out for you." Jed stripped off his sweater then unbuttoned his white shirt. "But in the meantime, I have something upstairs I'd like to introduce you to."

Dumping his bag with no thought for the contents, Jonty shot up the stairs, taking them two at a time. He hurtled into the bedroom, almost falling in his haste to strip off his clothes. He sat cross-legged on the bed then got both hands around his aching dick before Jed even made it into the room. It was a few minutes before Jed appeared.

"Hands off!" Jed growled. "I don't believe I said you could touch."

Pouting, Jonty sat on his hands. He couldn't trust himself to be obedient otherwise. He drank in the sight of Jed's bare chest and for the millionth time wondered at how lucky he was that this beautiful man wanted him.

"And now we have a bit of a problem, don't we?"

"We do?"

Jed laid a shiny metal tube on the bed. "I can't get you into this when you're in that condition, now can I?"

This proved to be a steel chastity tube. Jonty thought it looked menacing just lying on the covers. He couldn't imagine what it was going to feel like once he was trapped inside it. He shivered. *Perhaps if I stay hard long enough, Jed will get bored and forget about it.* "That's a shame. Maybe another time."

Jed shook his head. "It's a good job I came prepared. He had a small Ziploc bag in his hand. "He shook the contents out onto the bed. "These are rubber-lined cock rings. They've been in the freezer."

Jonty edged further away, eyeing the innocent metal circles with suspicion.

"They're hinged. One fits just beneath the head of your cock, one at the root and one around the base of your balls. I think they'll deal very nicely with your current…excitement." Jed picked up the largest of the three rings. "Lie down. Hold the headboard and keep your hands there. No wriggling."

"But…" Jed's expression told Jonty that compliance was his best option. He flopped down on his back with a sigh. "This is soooo unfair."

"You'll do it because I want you to. I haven't heard your safe word." Jed unhinged the ring. He gave Jonty's rigid cock a stroke then placed the metal around the base of his balls. Jonty squealed.

"That's cold! Oh my God!" He drummed his heels on the bed.

"Do I need to tie you down?" Jed raised an eyebrow.

"No, Sir. Well, maybe?" The proposal had some merit. Jonty loved bondage. Two minutes later his wrists were firmly bound to the brass rails at the head of the bed and his legs spread wide, each ankle securely tied. He was helpless, exposed and far too turned on for what Jed had in mind.

"Hmmm." Jed fixed the second ring just below the head of Jonty's dick. The final one encircled him at the root of his shaft. He tried to keep still, he really did, but the intense cold sent spikes of pain through parts of his anatomy he preferred to keep safe. His erection wilted. "That was effective," Jed commented as if he hadn't just tortured his boyfriend.

"No kidding!" Jonty exclaimed. "Get these things off of me, Jed…please."

"My wish is your command." Jed removed the rings only to replace them with the chastity tube, which encased Jonty's dick completely. He secured the thick ring holding it in place with a small padlock, which hung like a weight beneath his balls.

"This isn't really what I had in mind." Jonty strained to see.

"Is there any pinching, any sore points?" Jed ran his finger around the edges of the metal and Jonty's cock made a valiant attempt to swell.

"No! And you're not helping." Jonty squirmed as much as he was able.

"You mean you don't want me to do this?" Jed cupped Jonty's balls, stroking with the pad of his thumb.

"No! Yes! No… I don't know!" He had no idea why he was so turned on. Jed had taken away his ability to come. He had control over Jonty's body and the part of his mind governed by the need to orgasm but instead of frustration, Jonty found himself floating on a wave of excitement.

"The point is," Jed said, "that you don't need to know. What happens to you is decided by me." He released Jonty's bonds. "Hands and knees."

Being ordered to do something was a relief. Jonty rolled over, praying that his muscles would hold him up. When Jed opened him up with a lube-slicked finger, he moaned as sensations he couldn't respond to rolled through him. Jed found Jonty's prostate and rubbed, turning him into a quivering ball of need. His cock, desperately trying to swell within the confines of its prison, ached.

"Jed! Please…need you."

"You'll get me…when I decide." Jed removed his probing finger. He climbed onto the bed, shunting Jonty over. "Undress me."

Jonty loved that suggestion. Jed only had his trousers on and they were soon removed to reveal close-fitting shorts. Taking a chance, Jonty nuzzled Jed's barely restrained erection. He smelled so good, Jonty was desperate for a taste. He slipped a finger beneath the waistband of Jed's underwear, peeling the garment down slowly, relishing the big reveal. Jed's cock sprang free, bounced a little then settled into an upright position. Jonty wasted no time pulling the irritating shorts down to his ankles so that Jed could kick them away. Jonty straddled Jed's lap, giving him the most appealing look he could manage. He didn't dare go further without permission.

"Hands behind your back. What you do with your mouth is up to you." Jed grinned. Jonty gripped his left wrist with his right hand. He shifted his knees for better balance and the glint of the chastity tube caught his eye. He scowled at it before catching Jed's smirk.

"You're enjoying this, aren't you?" He was curious.

"That you trust me this much? Yes."

Jonty dipped his head to lap at the tip of Jed's dick. Salt flavor burst over his tongue. "You taste good." He licked some more and Jed gripped the sides of the mattress. Inside, Jonty smiled. He loved that he could have such an effect on his big, strong lover. Jed's usual demeanor was stoic with a hint of mischief and Jonty wanted to make him fall apart. Covering his teeth with his lips, Jonty took most of Jed's length into his mouth. He eased forward in small increments, not wanting to gag, until Jed's tip hit the back of his throat. He swallowed. Jed groaned. Smiling, Jonty shifted back, pressing his lips around Jed's girth. He was aware of his own cock, fighting its imprisonment, but it didn't matter. He was able to focus on Jed's pleasure alone, liberated from his own need. He gripped his wrist tightly, bound by Jed's word, and sucked hard, relishing the soft skin over its hard core. His jaw ached and his lips were getting sore but he knew that Jed was getting close from the slight tremors in his muscles.

"Stop, Jonty."

Confused, Jonty let Jed's shaft slip from his mouth.

"I want to be inside you when I come. Put a condom on me."

It was strange to have the use of his hands back. Fingers trembling, Jonty grabbed a foil square from the bedside cabinet. He ripped it open then slid the gossamer fabric over Jed's shaft with some regret.

"We'll get tested soon. Be done with them."

"Can you read my mind?"

"Love, the goings on inside your head are a mystery to me. Now ride me. Hands…"

"Behind my back. I know." Jonty got into position over Jed's erection then sank down. The slight burn of penetration was overcome by pleasure as Jed's cock filled him. He threw his head back and clenched his inner muscles.

"Fuck, Jonty!" Jed grasped his hips. He traced the crease between Jonty's thigh and belly, making him squirm, then lifted him a few inches. Jonty became pliant in Jed's hands. He took some of his weight on his knees but apart from that Jed had control. Jed moved him up and down, faster and faster. Jonty watched Jed's muscles flex, mesmerized by his strength. He never felt safer than when he was in Jed's hands.

Even with the latex barrier between them, when Jed came, Jonty's passage filled with heat. Jed's gaze was firmly fixed on him and nothing in the world could make Jonty look away. His wrist ached he was gripping it so hard. He didn't want to move. The comfort of having Jed's cock inside him was difficult to explain so when Jed lifted him clear, he whimpered at the loss. Jed laid him on his back then dealt with the condom. When he returned, he used his key to unlock the padlock on the chastity device. When the metal sleeve was removed, Jonty shivered as cooler air hit his skin. He hardened so fast it had to be some kind of record, then the wet heat of Jed's mouth covered him. He lasted less than ten seconds before Jed's clever tongue brought him to orgasm and pinpoints of light filled his vision.

He might have blacked out for a few seconds, Jonty wasn't sure, but when he regained enough sense to realize what was going on—Jed was wiping him clean. Then he locked the chastity device back in place.

"What are you...?" Jonty was silenced by a kiss. A long, deep, tender kiss that made him forget the question he'd meant to ask.

"Would you like to sketch me now?" Jed climbed back onto the bed. He sat against the headboard, one knee raised.

"Yes!" Jonty scrambled to fetch paper and pencils. It didn't matter that he was naked. It mattered even less that his dick was encased in metal. What mattered was that he had Jed all to himself, that there was a delicious ache inside him from their lovemaking, and that just for a few minutes Jed was his to command.

Jed soon decided that Jonty should always sketch naked so long as he wasn't on public view. In fact, clothes should always be optional for him in the house. He had the sweetest lean muscles and his limbs were coated in downy blond hair that caught the sunlight, making it appear as if he were glowing. Every now and then he would ask Jed to change position — turn his head an inch to the right, lift his chin or lower a shoulder. He frowned as he worked, sometimes chewing the end of his pencil, occasionally holding it up to judge scale. At least that's what Jed assumed he was doing.

"Are you measuring the size of my dick?" Jed gave Jonty a fake scowl.

Jonty giggled. "Just making sure I get everything in proportion." He shifted position, sitting cross-legged at the bottom of the bed. "Perspective is very important."

"I hope these sketches aren't going into the auction." Jed made himself more comfortable against a pillow.

"These are for me!" Jonty exclaimed. "Nobody else gets to see your good bits." His pencil flew over the paper. "I want to do these in oils. They'll look fantastic."

Jed didn't attempt more conversation because he didn't want to distract Jonty and besides, there was something innately sexy about watching him work. He recognized the exact moment Jonty lost his concentration and began to worry. The furrows between his eyebrows deepened and some of the sparkle left his eyes. He stopped drawing, lowering the pad into his lap.

"What's wrong, sweetheart?"

Jonty blinked, his eyes filling with the gleam of unshed tears. "Why can't I get past it, Jed? Why can't I stay happy?"

Jed remained silent, waiting for Jonty to expand in his own time. He leaned forward to pat his bare knee.

"Every time I think I've moved on, the guilt creeps up on me. It's always a shadow in the room, you know, but I thought I'd consigned it to a dusty corner. I haven't. When I'm with you, I can forget the past but then it's as if I'm caught in a web. I manage to free myself for a while but then this malevolent spider starts to reel me back in. What's wrong with me, Jed?"

Jed pulled Jonty onto his lap. He held him tight so that Jonty's back was pressed against his chest then brushed his hair aside to kiss his neck. "You're still grieving and that's okay. There's no time limit on emotions. But you listen to me, Jonty — it is fine for you to be happy, just as much as it is for you to feel sad. You are *not* to blame for what happened to your family and I'd bet good money that none of them would want you to suffer because of what happened."

Jonty snuggled against him. "I know. I just need you to remind me."

"I'll tell you over and over but I want you to make me a promise."

"Okay."

"Whenever you get these bleak feelings, you will talk to me. If we're not together, you call me. If we're further apart, you get onto Skype. Any time of the day or night. And if I find out that you didn't get in touch for any reason — because you thought I was too busy or some such rubbish — I will spank that pretty arse of yours so hard you'll be carrying a pillow around with you for a month."

"You think I have a pretty arse?"

"Jonty…"

"Sorry. I hear you and I do promise. Cross my heart and pinky swear."

"That's better. Now finish those drawings. I have other nefarious plans for you tonight." He gave a B-movie villain laugh, making Jonty giggle.

"And will those plans involve freedom for my poor danglies?" Jonty gave the chastity tube a mournful glance.

"That's for me to know and you to wonder about." Jed slipped a hand beneath Jonty's balls then gave them a gentle squeeze.

Jonty squeaked. He scooted from Jed's lap, grabbed his pad then began to sketch. "Hmm, I'm going to have to alter these now." He gave Jed's lap a pointed stare. "Tormenting me seems to have a very interesting effect on you."

Jed gave his rigid erection a couple of strokes and smirked. Jonty stared, open-mouthed. When he got back to work he muttered under his breath — something about cruel dommy tops with sadistic streaks wider than the bay. Jed relaxed against his pillows, alert to

Jonty's mood but satisfied his head was back in a good place, just where Jed always wanted it to be.

Chapter Ten

"Jed! We're going to be late." Jonty hopped from one foot to the other.

Marmite cocked his head to one side, staring at Jed as if expecting an explanation. "Calm down. We have plenty of time to get to Kelly's." Marmite's ears pricked up at the mention of his favorite place.

"I can't calm down. This is the first time everyone involved in the auction is getting together and I have to talk to them. I feel sick."

"You don't have to do anything you don't want to do."

Jonty walked into Jed's arms. He needed his strength and comfort. "What would I do without you?"

"Probably starve in a garret somewhere, covered in paint." Jed hugged him tight. "If you decide not to say anything tonight, I'll do it for you."

"I love you so much." Jonty froze. "Oh…" The words he'd wanted to say for some time had slipped out. He buried his head against Jed's shoulder, letting his hair fall forward but Jed didn't allow him to hide. He tilted Jonty's chin, staring into his eyes.

"You love me?"

Jonty's face heated to furnace temperature. "I didn't mean to say it like that, I wanted it to be romantic but I haven't had the courage." The words came out in a rush.

"What could be more romantic than this?" Jed kissed him, long and slow. "I think I've loved you since the first moment I saw you in the water that awful day. The feeling has grown and grown but I wanted to hear it from you first. I thought I might scare you away if I came on too strong."

"You love me too?" Jonty's breath caught in his throat.

"More than I can say."

"Wow. Wait…what do you mean you saw me in the water?" Jonty's thoughts churned. "Oh my God! It was you that saved me. You were the rescue swimmer that got me out of the water." His heart pounded. "Why didn't you tell me?"

"Simple. I wanted you to like me for me, not because of what I did."

"I should be so mad at you." Instead Jonty kissed Jed over and over, covering his face as far as he could reach. "But that just makes me love you more."

Jed stroked his hair in the way that Jonty loved.

"Rescuing you was a team effort. I was just a small part of that and I didn't want it to color your feelings for me."

"Well, you succeeded. I love every bit of you. Though I have to admit your uniform is quite a turn-on." He rubbed his hardening erection against Jed's thigh.

"I thought we were going to be late?" Jed grabbed two handfuls of Jonty's ass.

"A few more minutes won't matter." Jonty dropped to his knees. He nuzzled Jed's denim-covered groin then lowered the zipper with care. "No underwear. Yum." He took Jed's shaft into his mouth, tasting his unique flavor. He sucked hard, drawing a groan from Jed, who grabbed Jonty's hair, holding him close. The pull on his scalp made Jonty suck harder. He adored the feeling of being held in place. He ran his tongue around the bulbous head of Jed's cock, a spot he knew was ultra-sensitive. Jed sucked in his breath then came in a rush, filling Jonty's mouth with salty heat. He swallowed, careful not to miss a drop, then licked Jed clean before tucking him back into his jeans. Jed pulled him to his feet.

"I'd return the favor, but I think you'll keep until later. I wonder how long you'll stay hard."

Jonty rolled his eyes. "Are you going to time me?"

"Quite possibly." Jed grinned. "At least your predicament will keep your mind off public speaking."

Jonty pulled his T-shirt down a bit further. It wasn't long enough to cover his embarrassment. "I should change."

"No time." Jed gave a short whistle to Marmite, who'd gone back to sleep in front of the Aga. "Don't worry, sweetheart, once you're sitting down no one will notice."

Marmite ambled over and immediately nosed Jonty's crotch.

"Well, almost no one." Jed let out a deep belly laugh.

Jonty pushed Marmite's head away. "You're supposed to be on my side, Marmite. Naughty dog."

He could have sworn the big dog grinned at him, tongue lolling. "He has your sense of humor."

"I think he loves you almost as much as I do." Jed stroked Marmite's glossy coat. "Now we really must go." He opened the door but took a step back. "Damn, it's raining. When did that start?"

Jonty peered into the gloom. "That's not rain, it's a monsoon!" The drops were pounding the ground so hard water was bouncing to knee level. "We're going to get soaked. I'll be surprised if anyone turns up for the meeting." He grabbed his waterproof from the hook behind the door. "Here, catch." He threw Jed's coat to him. "Maybe we should leave Marmite here?"

"If we leave him behind on a trip to Kelly's he'll never forgive us. Besides, his breed are water dogs, he'll be fine." Marmite, as if sensing the possibility he might be abandoned, was already out of the door and trotting toward the harbor.

"Guess he made up his own mind," Jonty said, stepping into the deluge. At least his coat was long enough to cover his erection. *Perhaps I can keep it on?* The problem was that as soon as he began to soften he remembered that Jed loved him and the problem came straight back again. He sighed. It wasn't a bad dilemma to have.

Outside, Jed grabbed his hand and together they ran most of the way to Kelly's. Marmite had beaten them to it and, though his coat was dripping, Kelly was at the door letting him inside.

"Quick, get in here. What a night!" Kelly ushered them into the warmth of the café. Jonty let the heat soak into him and tension dissolved from his hunched shoulders. He glanced around, astonished. Kelly had pushed his collection of mismatched tables into a rough rectangle, surrounded by chairs. At one end stood a caldron of soup, a pile of dishes and several baskets of crusty rolls. People were already clustered around the soup, from which wafts of tempting aromas issued.

"There's tea, coffee or chocolate on the counter." Kelly dragged Jonty's sodden coat from his shoulders. "Then my secret recipe chicken soup."

"Guaranteed to warm everyone up." Jed grinned. "Evening, everyone."

The chorus of responses didn't distract the crowd from the food and Jonty realized that he wasn't the center of attention. Marmite sat, tail brushing the floor, a hopeful expression on his face.

"Don't worry, Marm. I saved a big dish for you. Made it before I added the salt, so it's better for you." He laid a massive tureen on a mat near the door. Marmite looked at Jed. Jed only had to nod and Marmite's face was buried in the dish, happy slurping noises following.

"You spoil him rotten," Jed commented.

Kelly shrugged. "And you don't?"

Giggling, Jonty took a mug of chocolate then blew on it. It was steaming hot but when it cooled enough to sip he moaned as delicious chocolate silk slipped down his throat.

"You should only moan like that when you're naked in my bed," Jed whispered. "I'm going to make sure you do it again, later."

Jonty hoped the steam from his drink would be taken as the reason for his no doubt bright red face. That and wind burn from the run along the harbor. He scurried to the end of the table then took a seat, tucking his chair underneath as far as it would go so no one could see his lap. Jed brought him a bowl of soup, taking the seat next to him.

"Good soup?" Jed asked as Jonty guzzled his portion.

"Fantastic. Do you think Kelly would give me the recipe?"

"Not a hope in hell." Jed took a big slurp of his soup. "Unless I hold him down and you tickle him."

"I heard that!" Kelly sat on the opposite side of the tables. He banged his mug on the wood. "Come on, you layabouts, let's get this meeting started."

From beneath his lashes, Jonty checked who had turned out in the appalling weather. To his astonishment, half the village seemed to have shown up. There was the landlord from The Crusty Crab and Beth the barmaid, the vicar, Kennick and at least four members of the lifeboat crew, Steve, out of uniform, his leg now healed, and several of the local artists contributing pieces to the auction. Jonty chewed his lip. He clutched Jed's hand beneath the table.

"Hi, everyone, thanks so much for coming." He cleared his throat. "I uh...don't like talking much." That got him a few giggles and a lot of sympathetic glances. "But with only three weeks to go until the auction, I thought we should get together and pin down the final plans. Um...Kelly, you're in charge of refreshments...could you tell us what's been arranged?" Jed gave Jonty's knee a squeeze. His smile was full of pride.

"Sure." Kelly stood up. "And I don't have any problem speaking. So. We're all set for the big day. Saul has offered to man a barbecue so we can sell burgers and hot dogs to add to the funds. Charlie Settick at the butcher's will contribute all the meat and the bakery will donate the rolls. Sauce, onions et cetera will come from the village shop." He got a brief round of applause. "For the auction itself, The Crusty Crab will provide the booze and Kelly's" — he gestured around him — "will create posh finger food for the dignitaries. Oh, and the local branch of the WI have offered to do teas, cakes, squash for the littlies, that kind of thing. They just need a table and power for the water boiler."

Jonty was astonished at how generous people were being. He'd never dreamed Kelly would get so much organized in such a short time.

"And I'm happy to wrangle all the food and drink folk on the day, with Beth's help. Kelly's will be closed that day so no one can hide out in here." Kelly grinned. "I'll hand over to Kennick now." He sat down and the coxswain stood.

"The lifeboat station will be open all day and we'll be offering tours of the boat. Andy teaches at the local primary — he's offered to set up some craft tables for small kids, run a color in the lifeboat competition, that kind of thing. His wife does face painting, so expect an influx of Spider-Men, butterflies and cats, because those are her specialties." That got a round of applause. "We'll do some demos and throw a couple of the guys in the water a few times so we can rescue them. The kids love that."

Steve took his turn next. "I've enlisted some mates to keep an eye on the auction lots — not that I'm expecting trouble, but face paint and artwork don't mix. We also expect to take a lot of money over the course of the day and evening, so having a few coppers around should ensure no one gets tempted. There's a safe at the police house so I can look after the takings there until I can transport them to the bank."

"That's wonderful, Steve. Thanks." Jonty couldn't even remember asking him to sort out security arrangements.

Steve just nodded. "My pleasure."

Jonty stood up, knees shaking a bit. He didn't let go of Jed's hand. "We have almost two hundred lots for the auction." There was a collective gasp. "People have been so generous and my agent in London has been doing the rounds collecting donations. We are going to have a lot of visitors and I think every hotel room within a fifteen-mile radius is booked. Jed is going to be our auctioneer." Catcalls and heckling filled the room. "The auction itself will be in a marquee because there isn't enough room in the lifeboat station. Um…what else?"

"Publicity," Jed suggested.

"Oh… I…" Jonty's face heated.

"I'll cover that, shall I?" Jed stood and Jonty collapsed into his chair. "News has gotten around, that's for sure. We have local and county press coming along, local radio are sending a radio car and TV news are interested too. Jonty has had calls from some arts publications who may also show up. Everyone we know has been posting leaflets everywhere we can legally stuff them and posters are up in the local stores. Our neighboring lifeboat stations are also helping out just like we always do for them…" Jed was interrupted by the sound of beeping from several places around the room. It took Jonty a while to register that the noise came from pagers going off.

"Well, damn." Jed leaned down to give Jonty a kiss. "Seems like I've got to go, love. You gonna be okay?" Several men headed for the coat hooks.

"Of course." Jonty didn't feel nearly as certain as he made himself sound. "Go save people."

"I love you." Jed said it loud enough for everyone to hear.

"Me too," Jonty whispered. "Be safe."

Jed and the other crew members trooped out of the door into what was now a howling gale, providing sound effects to accompany the lashing rain.

Marmite wandered over to Jonty. He laid his head on Jonty's lap, snuffling his affection. Jonty scratched behind Marmite's ears and whispered a heartfelt prayer for Jed's safe return. *I will not cry. I will not cry.* He rubbed the back of his hand across his eyes, blind to the other people in the room. Someone squeezed his shoulder and he remembered he wasn't alone.

"He'll be fine, Jonty. They'll all be fine." He wasn't sure who spoke but he hoped the words would prove prophetic. Jed loved him. He'd come back. He had to.

* * * *

Half an hour later, Jonty and Marmite followed Steve into the lifeboat station. They'd seen the boat launch as they fought the wind and rain along the bay but it had soon been lost to the darkness and towering surf. Soaked to the skin, Jonty clamped his lips together in an attempt to stop his teeth chattering. If the weather was this bad on land, he could only imagine how bad it must be at sea.

Marmite, appearing unperturbed by his soggy state, did a full body shake. Water droplets went everywhere, including all over Jonty.

"Like I'm not wet enough, Marm!" Jonty caught an old towel that Steve threw at him.

"Rub him down a bit, then go use the showers, Jonty. There will be spare clothes in Jed's locker you can use." He headed toward the door to the break room and office. "I'm going to get in touch with the coastguard and let them know we're on the radio. Find out what the emergency is."

Getting Marmite a bit drier was a useful distraction. Jonty gave him a thorough rub-down, which finished with Marmite rolling on his back with his legs in the air. As soon as his undercarriage had been dried to his satisfaction, Marmite made his way to his blanket pile in the corner of the break room, turned in several circles then lay down and went to sleep, nose on paws. Jonty shook his head. If only he could be so calm.

He followed Steve's advice and wandered through to the locker room. He stripped off his sodden clothes, leaving them in a bedraggled heap on the tiled floor. He soon had the shower room full of steam but when he stepped beneath the spray it felt as if the water was scalding his skin. He knew it was his body temperature that was the problem rather than the spray and soon he warmed enough to enjoy the heat. He hadn't thought about a towel so when he was done, he had a short, cold run to the changing area to find one. Inside Jed's locker there were three dry towels and two sets of clean clothes. Jonty wrapped himself in one of the towels then sat on the bench. He took a few deep breaths in an attempt to calm down and clear his head. He had to learn not to react so strongly every time Jed was called out, otherwise he'd be a nervous wreck.

"He's well trained and it could be a false alarm. It's probably nothing." Outside, the wind screamed. "Not helping," Jonty muttered.

"Talking to yourself?" Steve came into the room. "First sign of madness, you know." He proceeded to strip. "Ironic, isn't it—needing to get wetter before we get dry."

"What did the coastguard say?" Jonty asked.

"Not enough. A flare was sited from the cliffs between here and Newquay. They've sent our boat and Newquay's. They know of two yachts that should be in the area and can't make radio contact with either of them. That's all I know." He loped into the showers, yelling when the water hit his skin for the first time.

Jonty giggled. "You sound like I did five minutes ago," he shouted, trying not to think about the possible implications for the missing yachts.

"That's it—laugh at my pain. What kind of friend are you?"

While Steve showered, Jonty dressed in Jed's clothes. The sweats, T-shirt and pullover were all far too big but he rolled the cuffs and tucked the trousers into Jed's woolly socks. He was soon toasty warm and calm enough to do something useful. He gathered his discarded clothes, wondering what to do with them. Steve appeared, a towel wrapped around his hips.

"There's a tumble drier in the break room. You can shove that lot in there. Can you put my stuff in too?"

"Sure." With an armful of wet clothes, Jonty went to find the drier. He got it going then put the kettle on. He was British. Tea was essential. He found a teapot, milk, mugs and an unopened packet of Jaffas. As he was setting things out on the table, two women burst into the room, shedding wet coats as they came.

"Now, will you look at that, Essie? A man who knows how to brew a decent cuppa. You must be Jonty, Jed's boyfriend?"

Jonty nodded, feeling shy. He was enveloped in a hug, his senses overwhelmed by the scent of sandalwood. "Um…hi?"

"Don't mind me, love. I'm Kennick's long-suffering wife, Carole. This is Andy's other half, Essie."

"You're not scaring him, are you, Carole?" Steve arrived and gave both women hugs. "I found Mungo in the locker room. He took an unhealthy interest in my towel." A golden retriever circled the table, tail wagging. He went over to Marmite, gave him a lick then settled down on the blanket next to him. Marmite opened one eye and surveyed the room before going back to sleep.

While Steve repeated the little information he had about the shout, Jonty carried on making tea, finding two more mugs. Over the next half an hour, he had to find several more until there were twelve adults, three children, one baby and five dogs crammed into the room. Jonty picked a chair at the corner of the table and tried to be invisible. The Jaffas disappeared in seconds but everyone who arrived seemed to have brought food and the table was laden with home-baked cakes, sandwiches and sausage rolls. Even Marmite couldn't sleep through the racket but he was great at amusing the children and managed to hoover up discarded scraps whenever they hit the floor. Shadow, a border collie, kept trying to round up the toddlers while Sally, a cocker spaniel, was clearly in love with Marmite. A nameless Westie puppy sat in Jonty's lap, giving his hand an occasional slurp—Jonty had no idea who he belonged to, but he was white, fluffy and adorable. Apart from Steve, the only other man in the room was Sara's partner and he seemed well used to storm gatherings and knew everyone. Jonty stroked the puppy in his lap and prayed he wouldn't be asked to hold the remarkably placid baby that was being passed around the table for cuddles.

As if sensing his discomfort, Steve put a pile of paper and some pencils in front of him. "I stole the paper from the printer. Thought you might like to sketch."

It was a huge relief to have busy hands. He drew each of the dogs first, handing the sketches to their owners, blinking away the compliments that followed. Then he did the kids, much to the delight of their mothers. Then the adults wanted portraits too. Jonty was delighted that his doodling kept all their minds off the danger their loved ones might be in.

It had just passed midnight when Steve went to get an update from the coastguard. Jonty's stomach knotted and the Westie, as if sensing his anxiety, snuffled in his sleep. Jonty stroked his soft fur, marveling at his tiny paws and velvet ears. It would be hard to give him back.

When Steve returned, a serious expression on his face, the chatter died down and several sets of expectant eyes turned to him.

"The news is sketchy but they are on their way back. Coastguard has two ambulances heading our way for casualties…and before you ask"—he held up his hands—"I don't know who they are or what condition they're in. They're bringing them in here because the bay is more sheltered than at Newquay, but comms between the boat and shore are poor because of the weather."

"How long?" Carole asked.

"An hour, tops."

Steve's announcement instigated a flurry of activity as preparations were made to feed the hungry returning crew. Taking the sleeping puppy with him, Jonty slipped from the room. He found himself a quiet spot on top of a coil of rope in the boatshed. The doors were closed because of the wind but it was still cold. He made sure the puppy was safely wrapped in a fold of Jed's voluminous sweater then leaned against the wall to wait.

Chapter Eleven

Jed pushed away the weariness that threatened his concentration. He needed to be focused to get the boat into the harbor. Seven rescued sailors and his entire crew were relying on his skills. It had been a hellish few hours. Back in the cabin, Jed had left Kennick sucking down gas and air, his suspected collarbone fracture causing him no small amount of pain. There was also a body bag on the floor of the cabin. One of the sailors on the floundering vessel had had a heart attack before they'd even arrived.

Jed gripped the wheel so hard his knuckles went white. He couldn't get the events of the night out of his head. In all his years on the boat, only one other shout had been worse and that had involved Jonty. Jed thumped the wheel—at least back then they'd had decent information about what was going on. This shout had been vaguer than a press release from MI5. They'd traveled a mile out to sea, battling some of the biggest waves Jed had ever experienced, then worked a line parallel to the shore with the Newquay boat doing the same from the opposite direction. Two hours later, by luck more than judgment, they had found a drifting yacht, its main mast gone. Alongside it was a life raft from another yacht that had already gone down.

Retrieving seven traumatized sailors and one body from the two vessels had been dangerous work. Kennick had been thrown against the rail and had fallen badly. Jed had a cut above his eye that he could no longer feel but probably needed stitches. Andy had bruised ribs and Jeannie had gone overboard at one point and had had to be hauled back by her safety line. As the last survivor had made it onto the lifeboat, the second yacht had tipped then slid beneath the waves. It had taken less than ten seconds to disappear.

As the *Govenek* crested a wave, Jed spotted lights in the distance. He used the intercom to let the crew know they would soon be home then put all his attention on getting past the breakers to the relative safety of the harbor. A wall of water buffeted the boat sideways and he fought to retain control. There was nobody on shore to rescue the rescuers if they went over. It took five minutes of battling the wheel before he finally made it past the breakwater. At last, the waves calmed. Rain still lashed the screen but the worst was over. Maneuvering the boat toward the slipway was something Jed could do in his sleep. He dropped anchor with a sigh of relief. One of the others would organize disembarkation before the boat could be hauled back up the launch slipway.

Despite the hour, there was a crowd of family on the dock. Jed couldn't see Jonty and a vague sense of disappointment flooded through him — until he walked through the boatshed doors. Jonty sat on a huge coil of rope, Marmite lying next to him. Jed recognized the jumpers and sweats Jonty was wearing as his own. A tiny, white furry face peeked from beneath the hem of the sweater. Jonty had his eyes closed and seemed to be muttering something under his breath.

"Jonty?"

Lashes lifted to reveal Jonty's pretty green eyes. "Jed!" Jonty launched himself across the room, cradling the dog. For some reason he didn't have shoes on, just woolly socks. Jed wanted to hug him but didn't want to crush the puppy. A crowd of people passed them, heading for the break room.

"Could you take…?" Jonty handed off his burden to Angela, the puppy's owner.

"Thanks for looking after him, Jonty. You know he has several litter mates looking for homes — you should come visit them at the farm. Give me a call, okay?"

Jonty nodded, "I'd love that!"

"He's not as cute as you." Jed wrapped Jonty in a hug.

"That's such a lie!" Jonty exclaimed. "He's adorable. I wanted to come outside with the others, but I couldn't. Steve said people were hurt. I couldn't bear for it to be you. I'm sorry…"

"There's nothing to apologize for, and I'm fine. It was a bad night, love. I want to go home and be with you, alone. Is that okay?"

"Of course." Jonty looked up at him. "You *are* hurt! You're bleeding. Jed, you need to get that cut seen by someone."

"A few butterfly bandages will deal with it just fine. You can nurse me better."

Jonty's cheeks gained an appealing blush. "Wait here. I'll fetch my clothes and things. Then we can go. I think

Marmite needs some doggy time." Marmite was leaning against Jed's leg, giving him an adoring look, tongue lolling.

Jed knelt on the floor, almost too tired to stand. He cuddled Marmite, giving him lots of strokes and reassuring words. "So, did you see that puppy, Marm?" Marmite snuffled against him. "You were a cute baby too, you know?" Jed scratched behind Marmite's ears. "I think some company for you might be a good idea. No saying anything to Jonty, though. Got it?" Marmite barked. "Good."

Jonty reappeared, laden with clothes and bags. "Hey. The ladies insisted I take some food for you. There's enough here to feed a small army."

Jed took a few things from him. "It will keep until tomorrow. I'm too tired to eat. So tired, in fact, that if Marm was a bit bigger I might be tempted to ride him home." Marmite gave him an indignant stare and he found the energy to laugh.

Jonty grabbed his hand, giving it a tug. "Come on, you're too big for me to carry either. The sooner we get home, the sooner I can tuck you into bed."

It gave Jed a warm feeling to hear Jonty refer to the cottage as home. He let him lead the way across the harbor and hardly noticed the driving rain. The three of them stumbled into the kitchen, dripping.

"I can't believe I got wet all over again," Jonty complained, stripping to his underwear in the middle of the kitchen.

Jed's cock made a valiant attempt to rise but, to his disgust, exhaustion won out.

"Come on, dump your wet things. We can clear everything up in the morning." He checked his watch. "Well, later in the morning. It's already tomorrow."

"I'm ordering a lie-in for all of us. No alarms. No crack of dawn walks. Sorry, Marm." Jed peeled damp clothes off, dropping them in a pile. "Even my shorts are wet."

"Take them off, then." Jonty leered.

"You first."

Jonty wiggled out of his skimpy briefs then ran for the stairs. Jed kicked off his shorts. He ran after Jonty, chasing the tempting pale glow of his ass. When he got to the bedroom, Jonty was already scrambling into bed. He held up the covers in invitation. Jed dived beneath them. He pulled Jonty to him, shifting until Jonty's ass fit snug against his groin and his back was pressed to Jed's chest. He wrapped an arm around him, holding him tight.

"Love cuddling," Jonty murmured.

Jed was asleep before he could even think about answering.

* * * *

The following morning, Jonty woke to find himself alone. He patted Jed's side of the bed but the sheet was cold. He peered over the side of the mattress but there was no sign of Marmite either. There were traces of blood on Jed's pillowcase and Jonty realized he'd not attended to the cut on Jed's brow the previous evening. In the bathroom he found a damp towel and signs that the shower had been used—the scent of Jed's favorite gel was still in the air. At the realization that morning sex and shower sex were both off the menu, Jonty went through his morning routine with a slight pout. He had no idea how Jed had managed to sneak out of bed without him noticing. When he went back to the bedroom to dress he glanced outside and was glad to see the sun out. He dressed in warm clothes, intending to get some more sketching done before he headed back to Cliff House to finish his painting for the auction.

In the kitchen there was no evidence of cooking, just a single cereal bowl on the drainer. Jonty pushed the workshop door only to find it blocked. A glimpse of dark fur told him Marmite was acting as a draft excluder on the other side.

"Jed?" he called through the crack. "Are you in there?"

There was some noise, then shuffling. "Move your hairy backside, Marm." Jed opened the door. "Good morning, gorgeous. Did you have a nice lie-in?"

"It would have been better with you." Jonty accepted a kiss.

"I know. Sorry. I have a load of work on and I wanted to spend some time on my auction sculpture first."

"That's okay. I'm just being selfish." Jonty tried to peer around Jed's body. "Can I see it?"

"No. Not till it's finished."

"Can I bribe you with bacon?" Jonty was desperate to see Jed's work. At the word *bacon*, Marmite barged through the door into the kitchen.

"Not me, but my door guard is more easily corrupted it seems. What are you planning this morning?"

"I've finished the watercolor series for the auction but I also have an oil that I want to enter. It needs some final touches so I'm going to do that. Would you like me to take Marmite for a walk after I've eaten or have you two already been out?"

"I came straight in here. Just had a cup of tea and a bowl of cornflakes. If you don't mind taking him, that would be great. I was going to take a break to walk him but that would let me get on while I'm in the swing of things."

"Okay. I'll bring him back before I go up to Cliff House. He'll just get bored there."

Jonty let Jed get back to work. He made himself a quick bacon sandwich with far too many extra rashers for Marmite.

"You'd qualify as a stage magician, the way you made those disappear, Marm. We'll have to walk further now to work off the calories." Jonty cleaned up the kitchen then grabbed his jacket. When he stepped outside, he was glad he had it. The sun was out but there was a sharp bite to the wind. He set off in the direction of the lighthouse but Marmite had other ideas, following the route Jed usually took. Jonty had to jog after him.

"Slow down, you daft dog! You know I don't like walking along the beach without Jed." Marmite kept going. Jonty sighed and trudged after him. He kept well back from the water, eyeing the cresting waves nervously. There were a few other people on the beach—more dog walkers at the far end, two pensioners sitting in deckchairs sharing a flask of something that steamed and a family with three young children exploring the rock pools. Jonty watched them, listening to their excited shouts, rather than looking at the ocean. He found the motion of the water hypnotic and it often sent him back to that day at sea, trying to keep his balance on a rolling yacht. Marmite brought him a stick, tail wagging, so he threw it as far as he could. Marmite lolloped after it, nosing through seaweed at the tideline to retrieve his prize. He brought the stick back, and dropped it at Jonty's feet, but as Jonty bent to pick it up he realized something was wrong. One of the small children by the rock pools had wandered away from her family and they were so engrossed in their treasure hunting that they hadn't noticed. The child toddled into the water and to Jonty's horror was knocked down by a wave. He fixed his gaze on the flash of pink and sprinted down the beach, stripping his coat off as he went. Marmite bounded alongside him. There was a scream as one of the child's parents realized what was happening.

Jed had told Jonty that the cove shelved steeply beneath the water. The undercurrent would pull the child out to sea in no time. He yelled as a blonde head bobbed in the water then disappeared beneath the surface. He ran as far as he could then dived forward over a breaking wave, aiming for the last place he saw the toddler. Pain flashed through his body as his nerve endings registered the cold but he powered forward, driven by an all-consuming need to find the child. After a quick glance around, he dove under and a flash of pink caught his eye. Reaching out, he grabbed at the color and his fingers found fabric. He fought to the surface, dragging his burden. As he broke through, he hauled the little girl with him. She didn't seem to be breathing. Jonty had no idea how he was going to fight the current and get her to shore, but then Marmite appeared next to him. He held on to the dog's scruff and Marmite towed him and the child toward the beach. As soon as his feet touched pebbles, Jonty struggled upright. He got clear of the waves, laying the child down on the ground. Gasping for breath, he tilted her head, checked her airway then began mouth to mouth.

"Let me!"

Jonty rolled to one side as the child's father took over and seconds later the girl coughed then brought up some water. When she started crying, Jonty knew she'd be okay. He realized he was crying himself, one hand tangled in Marmite's soaking fur. A wave rolled over his feet and he scrambled away in panic. His clothes were so heavy with water that he could barely drag himself to his knees. Pebbles dug into his flesh with bruising ferocity. His teeth chattered.

"You saved her life! Thank you. Thank you so much. You're both heroes."

Jonty didn't feel like a hero. The screech of a siren sounded from beyond the harbor wall. Jonty could just see the roof of Steve's police car, then Steve tore down the beach, sliding on the pebbles. "Get her into the car—it'll be quicker for me to take her to the hospital rather than waiting for an ambulance to get down here," Steve ordered the girl's father.

"Emily. Her name's Emily." Cradling the child, her father raced toward the car.

"You okay, Jonty?"

"Go! Look after the kid." Jonty staggered to his feet. He watched Steve and the rest of Emily's family make it to the car. They packed themselves in then Steve took off toward the village, lights flashing. A small crowd had gathered, no doubt drawn to the commotion, but Jonty brushed off their congratulations and well wishes—he just wanted to get home. The quarter-mile walk felt like an endurance march but as Jonty reached the ramp leading off the beach, Jed appeared at the top. Jonty staggered but Jed was there to catch him and hold him up.

"So, I hear you and Marmite took an unscheduled swim."

Jonty's teeth were chattering so hard he couldn't answer. He managed a weak smile.

"Oh, love…"

Jonty burst into tears. Jed scooped him up then carried him the rest of the way home while Jonty buried his face against Jed's chest and sobbed. In the warmth of the kitchen, Jed put Jonty down. "You're freezing. Your lips are turning blue."

Jonty stood, unresisting as Jed stripped his sodden clothes off, dumping them in a pile.

"I'm all salty…"

"I'm going to run a bath. You need to soak in the warmth before you get hypothermic." He carried Jonty upstairs, wrapped him in a towel then sat him on the toilet while he ran hot water into the tub.

"How did you know…?"

"Steve rang me. Told me I have a genuine hero on my hands."

"Marmite did most of the work. I wouldn't have made it without him."

"Well, he'll get a bath too, but he's built for cold water and you're not, so you get first go."

"This is the third time I've gotten wet today. It's getting to be a habit." Jonty dipped a toe in the water. "It's scalding!"

"No it's not, but your body temperature is so low it feels that way. Just take it slow."

Jonty inched his way into the water. It took him almost ten minutes to get fully submerged and Jed held his hand the whole time. The warmth soaked through him and after a while he could relax his shoulders and his teeth stopped banging together. He dipped his head beneath the surface then shampooed to get rid of the salt. Jed held the shower while he rinsed out the suds.

"Feeling better?" There was something in Jed's tone that made Jonty sit up.

"Much, thanks."

"You and I are going to have a long conversation about you risking your life, Jonty." Jed handed him a towel. "I swear I'm never letting you out on your own again." As soon as Jonty had the towel wrapped around his body, Jed pulled him into a fierce hug.

"I'm... I don't really know how I am. Everything happened so fast. I didn't want to get into the water but I was closest. The little girl would have drowned. I couldn't let her die, Jed. I couldn't save my family but I *could* save her."

"I might have lost you... I don't know whether to kiss you or spank your arse."

"Well, both would be nice."

"I love you, Jonty. Don't ever do anything like that again."

"Says the man who faces Lord knows what every time the lifeboat gets called out."

"It's not the same thing."

"No. It's worse." Jonty met Jed's gaze. "I go out for a walk and there's a minute chance I'll get into trouble. You respond to a shout and there's every possibility you won't come back." His voice cracked. "But I won't ask you to give it up. Not ever. And I can't promise that I won't put myself in danger again."

Jed sighed. "I'm chaining you to the bed anyway."

Jonty giggled. "I have to paint and you have to work. Once I'm dressed I'll go to Cliff House like I planned. You can chain me to the bed tonight, okay?"

"Remind me again who's in charge in this relationship?" Jed bent to kiss him.

"You are, of course."

"Your mouth says one thing, your eyes tell another story." Jed shook his head. "I'm so screwed. Fine. Go paint. I need to bath Marm then get back to work. Call me when you get to Cliff House — and that's not a suggestion, Jonty, it's an order."

"Yes, Sir." Jonty toed the bath mat, his eyes cast down. "Give Marmite a treat for me? He deserves one."

"You know how much I want to drag you to the bedroom, right now?"

"If it's as much as I want to be dragged there, then a lot."

"Later." Jed edged out of the door. "That's a promise."

Jonty took a few slow breaths, listening as Jed descended the stairs. "A promise I'll make sure you keep, Jed Curnow." He couldn't keep the smile from his face.

Chapter Twelve

Jonty checked his watch. He'd been painting for hours but didn't want to lose track of time. His auction piece was finished and he was pleased with the result. He'd even had time to frame the series of watercolors he'd done on local life. The day had remained fine and the view from his painting room showed the sea glinting with gold. From a distance it was beautiful.

"Still don't want to get in it again," Jonty muttered. He cleaned the paint from his hands as best he could then went to find his shoes. In one more week the sale of the house would be complete and as he walked through to the kitchen, he experienced a pang of nostalgia. It didn't last long. His future was with Jed and for that he needed a clean break from the past. He grabbed his keys from the counter but a sound from outside distracted him. He peered out of the window — there was nothing out of place — but as he walked toward the front door he could see shadows beyond the frosted glass panels. As he approached, someone knocked. As soon as he opened the door, a camera flash went off in Jonty's face and he was assaulted by a barrage of questions. A microphone was shoved at him and he could make out at least half a dozen people.

"Jonathon Trelawn. Is it true you saved a child's life this morning? Are you hiding out here in Cornwall? Did today's events bring back memories of losing your parents?"

Jonty slammed the door. With shaking hands, he dialed Jed's number. Jed picked up immediately.

"Jed, the press are here. I can't leave. I don't know what to do."

"Calm down, love. There are people in the village asking questions too. I'll give Steve a call then we'll come get you. If they're on your property, they're trespassing if you don't want them there. Steve can move them on. Sit tight. I'll be there as soon as I can."

"Okay." Jed's voice infused Jonty with instant calm.

"There are TV crews down at the harbor — is there something I don't know about you, Jonty?"

"Um, well, I…"

"Never mind. It doesn't matter. I'm on my way."

Clutching the phone in case Jed called back, Jonty went back to his painting room. He lowered the blinds then sat on the floor against the back wall to wait. While he was sitting there, the phone rang again. He checked the number but it was Shaw calling from London.

"Hi, Shaw, this isn't the best time…"

"I have journalists calling me every fifteen seconds, Jonty. Is it true?"

"Is what true?"

"Don't be obtuse. Did you throw yourself into the sea to rescue some kid?"

"Yes…but…"

"I already had collectors screaming at me for your work. This makes you gold dust."

"I didn't do it for the publicity, Shaw. I was just in the right place to help and, besides, I had assistance."

"From a big cute dog. Jesus, Jonty that just completes the package as far as the papers are concerned."

"I don't want to talk to them. Can't you deal with it? Issue a release or something?"

"I can if you want me to, but think about it—this could be great publicity for the auction if you talk to them in person. Is your piece finished by the way?"

"Yes, it is, but…"

"Bidding will be frantic. I hope you've got online options because you'll have international interest."

"There's a website but it's just for the catalogue and details of times and location, that kind of thing. Bidding has to be in person or by phone."

"Are you in the Dark Ages down there? Damn. Well, I'll make sure there are plenty of my people with phones there on the day. Send me the link to the catalogue site when it's ready and I'll get word around."

"Okay, thanks. I'll think about making a statement or something but for now, I need to go. I think the cavalry has arrived." Jonty rang off then crept down the hall. He heard Steve ordering the journalists off the property but he still put the chain on the door before he opened it.

"It's us, sweetheart. You can let us in." Jed stood on the path, strong, certain with his big smile and twinkling blue eyes.

"You'd better have coffee in there, Jonty." Steve, in uniform, appeared at Jed's side. "You've caused more commotion around here in one day than I've had to deal with in months."

Jonty let them in. Steve headed straight for the kitchen in an impressive display of diplomacy while Jed pushed Jonty against the wall. He held his hands over his head then kissed him, long and hard. When he finally let go, Jonty leaned against him. "I love you. You always know what I need."

"I'm here now. Let's go get Steve his coffee."

Jonty loved that Jed could be so calm and matter-of-fact. He didn't interrogate or pry, just offered support without any other agenda. He followed him to the kitchen where Steve had already boiled the kettle and was scooping instant coffee into three mugs.

"Sorry there's no better coffee. The machine is packed in a box somewhere." Jonty leaned against the units, too disconcerted to sit without fidgeting.

"I don't care where my caffeine fix comes from, as long as I get it," Steve proclaimed as he handed out drinks. "Now. If I'm to keep fending off hordes of journalists, I need to know why they're all flocking around you like bees to a honeypot, Mr. Trelawn."

Jonty sighed. "It's easier if I just show you." He fiddled with his phone, bringing up a couple of websites. He handed it first to Jed, who read out the titles.

"Record-breaking price achieved for painting by young prodigy Jonathon Trelawn. Royal Academy exhibits painting by Jonathon Trelawn. *Arc Light* by Jonathon Trelawn wins Carstein prize." He handed the phone to Steve. "Seems we have a celebrity on our hands, Constable."

"Well, fuck me! You kept all this quiet, Jonty. Should I be asking for your autograph?"

Jonty, terrified that Jed might somehow see him in a different light, pressed against him. To his relief, Jed put an arm around his waist and squeezed.

"I just want to paint," Jonty whispered.

"This explains the level of fuss," Jed noted, "but remember you don't have to do anything you don't want to, Jonty. If you don't want to talk to the press, that's your decision."

"I can't think… I want to go home. Sorry—I don't want to sound like a petulant kid, but I hate when they hound me. I'm not a hero. Anyone on that beach this morning would have done the same thing and if it hadn't been for Marmite…" He bit his lip. "They just want to drag up the past."

"I can go back to the car," Steve said. "Tell them you won't be coming out tonight. That should give you enough time to take the back lane round to the road. You can walk down to Jed's without being seen. I doubt anyone in the village will tell them you live at Jed's place."

"It could work," Jed agreed. "We'll give you ten minutes then leave."

"I'll come by in the morning. Let me know then what you want to do, Jonty. I'll help any way I can."

"Thanks, Steve." Jonty gave him a hug.

"Hey, no smooching with men in uniform," Jed protested, pulling him back.

"Caveman."

"You know it."

Steve grinned. "I'll let myself out. See you in the morning."

* * * *

Jed guided Jonty through the back lanes to the harbor. They slipped through the rear entrance to the cottage without being seen by anyone except an uninterested tabby cat. Jed kept a firm hold on Jonty's arm every step of the way, not able to countenance letting go. Once they reached the security of the kitchen he relaxed, but he still locked the door. Marmite heaved himself up from his spot by the Aga to say hello. Jonty dropped to his knees, wrapping his arms around the big dog's neck. "Sorry, Marm, I didn't mean to bring so much excitement into your life."

"If the next words out of your mouth have anything to do with us being better off without you in our lives, I'm going to gag you," Jed commented. He pulled two bottles of beer from the fridge. "We deserve a drink." He popped the caps before handing one bottle to Jonty.

"I... You mean that, don't you?" Jonty took a long swallow.

Jed watched his Adam's apple bob. "Have I ever said anything to you that I don't mean?"

"I'm sorry."

"For what?"

"Being me. Having more baggage than Heathrow's lost property department."

"Finish your beer, Jonty."

As soon as they were done with their drinks, Jed herded Jonty upstairs. "Strip. Kneel on the bed, hands behind your back." While Jonty was taking his clothes off, Jed went to the chest of drawers. The bottom drawer held his toy collection and he knew just what he wanted. First a pair of velvet-lined cuffs, which he used to secure Jonty's hands behind his back. Then something he'd been saving for a special occasion. He held it out to show Jonty, whose eyes widened.

"This is a deep throat o-ring gag," Jed explained. "The ring sits behind your teeth and forms a nice tube for my cock. You won't be able to close your mouth or speak once it's in place."

"I don't think I'm going to like this." There was a pretty pink flush on Jonty's cheekbones.

"You're not supposed to. This is a punishment for even thinking I'd be better off without you. Your job, your success...they're not why I fell in love with you. The sooner you get that fixed in your head, the better." Jed strapped the gag in place, securing the buckle behind Jonty's head. "I'm going to put a bell ball in your hand. It replaces your safe word. Drop it and this stops—understand?"

Jonty nodded.

Jed stroked his cheek above the leather strap, giving him time to drop the ball if he wanted to. "Sit back against the pillows."

Jonty shuffled back and Jed undressed, keeping a careful eye on him. When he knelt across him, Jonty's mouth was at the perfect height for Jed's cock. Just looking at him, bound, with his lips stretched around the gag made Jed rock-hard but he caught a glint of something in Jonty's eye. He removed the gag and the cuffs.

"I don't understand. I didn't drop the ball," Jonty said, massaging his jaw.

"But you don't want this." Jed lowered Jonty to the bed, gathering him into his arms. "I'm going to hold you, then I'm going to make love to you. You're not going to argue with me." Jonty melted against him. Jed stroked the curve of his arse, letting his hand rest around one plump cheek.

"How did you know? I didn't mind...I want you to be happy."

"You're mine. I see you. You grant me power over your body — that's not something I'll ever abuse."

"I love you so much!" Jonty straddled Jed's thighs. "Can I?" He gripped Jed's shaft, positioning it beneath his hole.

"Lube and condom first." Jed groped beneath the pillow for the tube. He handed it over with a grin.

"We've had the test results, Jed. I want to feel you without a barrier."

Jed's breath hitched. He nodded. "You first, then me." Watching Jonty stretch himself with two lubed fingers made Jed even harder. Jonty's lips were parted, his expression one of intense concentration. When he applied a coating of slick to Jed's cock, it was all Jed could do not to come. "Not gonna last."

"Good." Jonty impaled himself. He held his hands together behind his back as if they were still shackled. "Oh...that's perfect."

The heat of Jonty's body around his cock, the sight of his rippling muscles as he moved, brought Jed to the edge in record time. He reached for Jonty's straining shaft. "Come with me, love." Jonty shuddered through an intense orgasm and Jed shot deep within him — the sheer joy of it making him laugh. Jonty collapsed onto him, panting.

"Keep the gag for another time, yeah?"

"Kinky little brat." Jed pulled the covers over them both. "Snuggling now, clean-up later." Jonty was plastered to his front, giving his neck light kisses.

"Yes, Sir. Whatever you say."

Jed closed his eyes. He was well and truly under Jonty's paint-stained thumb and it wasn't a bad place to be.

* * * *

Jonty awoke as the sun was rising. After quick showers the previous evening, he and Jed had fallen into bed without drawing the curtains and now the room glowed pink and gold with early morning light. Jed lay on his back, one arm flung over his head, the other hanging from the side of the bed. His chin was dusted with twenty-four hours' beard growth, giving him a dangerous look that pressed all Jonty's buttons. He snuck beneath the covers, wriggling down the bed until he was in a good position to take Jed's impressive morning wood into his mouth. Jed tasted of spice and salt, his skin warm and velvet-smooth. Jonty hummed as he sucked, taking Jed as deep as he could without gagging.

Jed parted his legs wider but gave no other indication that he was awake. Jonty decided to up the stakes. He suckled each of Jed's balls in turn, letting the weight rest on his tongue before playing a little. Jed's breathing quickened so Jonty went back to his cock, giving all his attention to the head. Jed growled then tangled his fingers in Jonty's hair, holding him in place.

"I haven't had coffee yet, Jonty. No teasing."

Jonty giggled. He started sucking again in earnest, reaching for his own dick at the same time.

"I hope you're not touching yourself without permission."

Jonty debated whether or not to stop but decided that what Jed couldn't see wouldn't hurt him. Seconds later he swallowed the gush of Jed's seed as he came. Jonty tried to stay quiet as his orgasm overcame him, but his breath came out in a rush. He stuck his head out from under the covers. "Good morning!"

"It certainly is." Jed rolled him onto his back, looming over him. "You think I don't know you came?"

"I…um… Did I?" He wiped his sticky hand on the sheets in an attempt to get rid of the evidence.

"You are overdue a spanking." Jed kissed him, taking the sting from his words, though Jonty suspected his arse would be stinging soon. "After I first met you at Kelly's, I daydreamed about bending you over a flat surface, tying your hands then reddening your backside. Tonight I'm going to live the dream."

Jonty gulped. "I have to think about that all day?"

"It'll take your mind off the press." Jed vaulted off the bed. "Have you decided what you're going to do about them?"

"Yes. I think so. But I need your help, and Marmite's." Right on cue, Marmite's shaggy head appeared around the door. "Do you think he was listening?"

"Let's just say it's a good thing he can't talk. You can tell me your plan over breakfast.

* * * *

An hour later, well fed but feeling a bit queasy, Jonty walked toward the lifeboat station to meet Steve. He focused his attention on Steve's panda car rather than the small but vocal group of people gathered in front of it. There were at least two TV cameras and boom mics that he could see. He hated talking in public but at least making the statement outside would reduce his claustrophobia and he'd be less likely to panic. Steve had borrowed a table and two chairs from the lifeboat station, positioning them so Jonty's back was to the sea and the low sun. He slipped into one of the chairs before the collection of reporters even noticed he was there. He wasn't surprised—he hadn't been photographed in public for some time, his hair was longer and he dressed like a local surfer on a bad weather day.

Steve directed a wink his way then banged on the table. He seemed to be relishing his new role in public relations. Jonty hid a smile.

"Mr. Trelawn would like to make a statement," Steve announced. "Be quiet or I'll arrest you all for disturbing the peace." That brought a smattering of laughter.

Jonty stood, clutching a piece of paper with a few short lines scribbled on it. He cleared his throat, wishing he'd thought to bring a bottle of water. "There are a lot of unsubstantiated rumors going around about my role in yesterday's rescue of a small child who fell into the sea just a few hundred yards away from here." Cameras clicked and flashed, distracting him. He blinked. "I'm sure you'll be glad to know that the little girl left hospital this morning and she's fine. However, I can't take credit for saving her. I did get into the sea, I did find her and get her head above the water, but we probably still would have drowned if it hadn't been for an unsung hero. I was on the beach yesterday morning because I was walking my...boyfriend's dog." There was a collective gasp as Jonty outed himself, not that he'd ever deliberately hidden his orientation, it just hadn't come up. "So it's really Marmite you should be writing about..."

As Jonty said Marmite's name, Jed walked out of the lifeboat station with Marmite at his side. Marmite's coat glowed and he wore a bright red bandana around his neck instead of a collar. Jed came and stood with Jonty, letting Marmite do his thing. Within seconds he had charmed the entire posse of hard-bitten journalists by nosing at pockets, head-butting thighs and slurping hands. He accepted pats and rubs like a star. For a while Jonty was forgotten. He slipped his hand into Jed's and held tight. After the brief respite, a barrage of questions started.

"Is this your boyfriend? How long have you two been together?"

"Did the rescue bring back memories of your parents?"

"Do you think you'll break records for the price of your next painting?"

Jonty ignored them. "I'm not answering questions this morning. My next work will be a lot in a charity auction to support the lifeboat station behind you. The crew here saved my life and this is my way of saying thank you. The local volunteer crew are the real heroes around here." Jonty steeled himself for a few photos of him, Jed and Marmite then sent Steve an appealing glance. Steve ushered the media toward the lifeboat station.

"We have a few crew members you can talk to if you'd like more information about the RNLI or the upcoming auction," he said, pacifying them.

Jonty and Jed waited until they were all inside.

"Can we go home now?" Jonty asked.

"We can. I didn't want them seeing where we live."

"I hope we gave them enough, now perhaps they'll leave us alone."

"I'm so proud of you." Jed put an arm around his shoulders.

"Marmite was the star. I hated every minute."

"It didn't show."

"Only because you were there with me." Jonty heaved a sigh of relief as they made it inside. Jed gave Marmite a good scratch and one of his favorite treats.

"Do you want to see my piece for the auction? It's finished," Jed asked.

"Yes!" Jonty bounced. "Of course I do. Wait — is this a distraction technique?"

Jed grabbed him before giving him a thorough kissing. "*That* was a distraction technique."

"It worked." Jonty's knees were jelly.

"I should hope so." Jed slid his hand down the back of Jonty's jeans. He gave his arse a squeeze. "You're not alone anymore, Jonty. I'm here for you. Always."

Jonty leaned against him. "I don't want to be some over-emotional, needy wreck."

"You're not. I'd guess you didn't enjoy media attention or crowds even before the accident."

"You're right. It was always something I endured rather than enjoyed. Shaw plays interference for me most of the time. He says being 'a pretty, emo, creative type with a tragic past' means I can hide and be mysterious."

"I can't wait to meet him, though I'm not sure whether I want to punch his lights out or shake his hand."

"I think you'll get on. He's protective too."

"Protective, me? Don't know what you're talking about." Jed rubbed Jonty's crease.

"So the whole 'chain me to the bed forever' thing isn't true?"

"Oh, it's true. In my perfect world you'd be naked, tied up and at my mercy twenty-four hours a day. But the world's imperfections make life interesting. I can spend my time plotting about *how* to get you naked, even when you're not." He leered.

"You're incorrigible." Jonty wiggled, trying to encourage Jed to move his finger some more.

"No lube."

"Don't care."

Jed sank a finger into Jonty's hole. He gasped and pressed against Jed's hard body. "Please, Jed. Need to come."

"Do you now?"

Jonty squirmed while Jed finger-fucked him. He ground his denim-covered dick against Jed's thigh, desperate for friction. When Jed found his prostate, Jonty yelped. His movements got more frantic. Coming proved to be joy, relief and ecstasy all rolled into one happy explosion of pleasure and when it was over, he sagged, exhausted. "Wow."

Jed chuckled. "Now you have to change before you can see my work."

"What about you?" Jonty scrabbled at Jed's fly but Jed moved his hand away.

"Later. I'm saving my energy for that spanking I promised you." Jed hugged him. "Now go take a shower. I'll see you in the workshop, okay?"

"Okay." Jonty's sticky walk upstairs made him smile. The day was turning out better than he could have hoped.

Chapter Thirteen

"That is absolutely incredible!" Jonty circled the sculpture in front of him, examining every angle. Carved from the piece of silver driftwood they had found on the beach, Jed had created an osprey in flight anchored to the sea by the tip of a single claw. The bird reached for the sky and in the wood that formed the base of the piece, the outline of a struggling fish could be made out amid the waves. "It's stunning. I knew your work was exceptional but this, this is on another level."

Jed's face heated. Such praise coming from the man he loved, a man who was a renowned artist, gave him chills. "You really like it?"

"I love it." Jonty snapped a picture with his phone. "I'm going to send this to Shaw. He'll warm the market up—make sure we get the very best price for it."

"Can't it just go into the catalogue like everything else?

"It will be in there, but Shaw is really good at generating interest. He'll circulate the picture to clients he thinks might like it then they'll either bid by phone or give him their proxy as he's coming along in person. He'll be doing the same for my picture as well."

"But you're a famous artist. I'm…"

"Brilliant. And undiscovered. That's enough to give some collectors an orgasm."

"The only person I want to give orgasms to is you."

That made Jonty giggle and blush. "And you do that so well."

Jed thrust his hands into his pockets. Jonty, with his pink cheeks and sparkling eyes, brought him close to losing control. He was tempted to throw his pretty man to the floor then fuck him senseless but he had work to do and so did Jonty.

Marmite wandered through the workshop, taking up his usual position near the front doors. "I think that's our signal to do something constructive." Jed covered his carving with a sheet. "What are you doing for the rest of the day?"

"I'm going to camp out at Kelly's and go through the whole auction plan, checking off all the details. Me, my phone and a few gallons of hot chocolate."

At the mention of Kelly's, Marmite barked. "Not you, greedy dog. You've had enough treats and attention for one day," Jed told him. Marmite rested his chin on his paws, looking disgusted. Jed checked his watch. "How about I meet you there for dinner around six?"

"Perfect. Have a good day." Jonty kissed him.

Jed sighed. Now he was hard again. "Get out of here, brat, before I do something you and I would both enjoy but won't help us get anything useful done."

Jonty pulled up the hood of his top, covering his distinctive hair. "Don't want to be spotted by any lingering journos," he said, then slipped out of the door with a brief wave. Jed resisted the urge to go after him and make sure he got to Kelly's without incident. He couldn't track Jonty every minute of the day, much as he'd like to. He'd be fine at Kelly's.

"Well, Marm, looks like it's just you and me for a while, and we have a couple of important jobs to get done." Jed turned the radio on then set to work. It wasn't a job for a client, but something much more personal that he'd been working on every time he had a spare half-hour. It was almost done and Jed was proud of how it had turned out. Two sloping wooden sides, fashioned from lacquered maple, were topped by a flat, padded surface upholstered in dark green leather. On either side, four smaller, padded shelves would provide support for Jonty's arms and legs. All Jed had left to do was attach the custom-made leather straps that would hold Jonty in place. As spanking benches went, it was state-of-the-art. Jed had even carved two intertwined Js on one side. Hinges allowed the sides to be folded for easy storage and Jed intended it should be given a home in the bedroom, where he hoped it would be in regular use. He sang along to soft rock while he worked, daydreaming about how Jonty would look laid out naked on their new toy.

Once he was done, Jed gave the bench a final check-over, running his hands over every surface. Any sharp edge or rough patch would have to be dealt with before he'd let Jonty anywhere near it but there was nothing. Jed hummed his satisfaction. He folded the bench then spent fifteen minutes getting it up the narrow stairs and into the bedroom. Once there, he set it up, debating whether to throw a cover over it. He decided to leave it on display. He couldn't wait to see Jonty's expression when he spotted it for the first time.

He made a quick sandwich for lunch, ate it then loaded the van with the new chopping block for delivery to the butcher's. Marmite rode shotgun, head out of the window, tongue lolling as the breeze ruffled his fur. After the block had been safely delivered and Marmite rewarded with some ham trimmings, Jed drove out of the village, heading for a dairy farm a mile or so away. He pulled into the yard and two collies and a Westie appeared from the milking shed, bouncing and barking. A man followed them out. Almost as big as Jed, he had a full beard and a mop of shaggy brown hair.

"Jed! What brings you out here?"

Jed got out of the van. "Hey, Bryan. I rang your missus about seeing the pups. Is it okay to let Marm out?"

"Sure. Keep the noise down, you mutts!" There was a cacophony of barking as Marmite joined the pack. They all tore off somewhere together to do whatever it was dogs did when they had a visitor. "She did mention it. Wasn't sure when you'd turn up, though. Come on into the kitchen — must be time for a tea break."

Jed had known Bryan since they were boys. They'd grown up together and trained alongside each other on the lifeboat. The farm, which Bryan had taken over from his parents, was a home from home.

"Angie not home?"

"She's in Newquay for the day, shopping." Bryan washed up at the sink before putting the kettle on. "Take the weight off."

Jed settled at the well-scrubbed table. "You know it's all her fault I'm here."

"I heard. Jonty is a firm favorite at the station. All the women love him. Angie even framed the sketch he did for her." Bryan pointed out the drawing, which had pride of place on a shelf above the Aga.

"He fell in love with the puppy she had with her that night and she mentioned you had a few looking for homes."

"Yeah, that one had been a bit poorly and she didn't want to leave it here. We've got three that don't have homes yet. It will be a few days before they can leave their mother—you saw her outside—so they're all still here at the moment, but to tell the truth I think she'll be glad to see the back of them. Get her bed back to herself." He handed Jed a mug of tea. "But you can have the pick of the rest."

"Great." Jed helped himself to a ginger nut from the packet Bryan put on the table. He dunked with care.

"What about Marmite, how does he feel about making room for a puppy?" Bryan asked.

"Marm has never met another animal he didn't like…apart from the cat that lives on Baker's Lane. I think the company will be good for him. I'm sure the pup will be bossing him around in no time."

"Well, they're in the utility, so as soon as you're done scoffing my biscuits, we can take a look, but be warned, they're so cute you don't stand a chance."

"Big, tough Bryan has been conquered by a bunch of fluff balls?"

Bryan shrugged. "Angie reckons I'm discovering my feminine side. I'll remind her of that the next time Brutus gets out."

"That bull is a psycho."

"Yep, but the girls love him and he makes good babies. Have you any idea how much quality bull semen sells for these days?"

"Time to visit those pups." Jed pushed his chair back. "You're touching on subjects I'd rather not explore."

Bryan fell about laughing. He led the way into the utility room where an area was blocked off for the puppies. Five sleepy balls of white fur opened their eyes. Jed had to admit they were adorable as they snuffled around on their piles of blankets, surrounded by toys.

"Which ones are still available?" They were hard to tell apart, though one was a bit smaller than the rest and had a black tip on one ear.

Bryan scooped up three puppies then handed them over. "These, but one's the runt."

Jed knew which one Jonty would choose, no question. "Which is the one we'll take." The puppies squirmed and licked. "I think one may have just peed on me."

"Quite likely. For small animals, they seem to pee gallons." Bryan laughed. "I'll hose you down in the kitchen."

"Thanks." Jed put the puppies back. "Will you be able to keep ours until auction day? I want to surprise Jonty at the end of the evening."

"Sure."

"What do I owe you?"

"Oh, we're not charging for them. We wanted to give Meggie a chance to have babies before she had the op. We didn't do it for money."

"I'll put something in the collection box at the station then."

Bryan helped Jed rinse his damp sleeve out. "You'd better get used to this — excited puppy equals pee, and they get excited a lot."

"I can handle it. Marmite as a puppy was eight times the size of this one. There's not much I don't know about the urinary habits of a dog. In fact, I think I still have some training pads left over somewhere."

"What are you going to call him?" Bryan asked.

"As if I'd dare choose. More than my life's worth. That decision sits with Jonty."

"Sounds like he's got you well under control. It's about time you found a good bloke."

"Just have to keep hold of him. I had no idea how famous he is."

"Don't you watch the news, Jed? Remember after we pulled him out of the sea, the fuss that was all over the papers?"

"I try to avoid reading or watching anything about rescues where there are fatalities. It's hard enough being there, I don't need to relive it with sensationalist spin added on the top." Jed frowned. "Jonty hates the attention. This auction he's arranging is turning into a really big deal. I'll be glad when it's all over and we can get back to our normal lives."

"Your normal is going to change when you become coxswain," Bryan said.

"What? Why would I..."

"Oh, shit. I thought you knew." Bryan looked sheepish. "Trust me to open my big mouth."

"What are you talking about? Kennick is coxswain. He'll be back as soon as his injury has healed.

"Kennick is retiring. His missus finally had enough — the collarbone was the last straw. She told him it was time to let go or he'd be sleeping on the couch. He's going to focus on training and imparting his wisdom to the rest of us poor sods."

"I had no idea." Jed didn't know what to say.

"You've been busy and I'm sure Kennick would want to ask you himself, so when he does, for Christ's sake act surprised, or I'll end up in the silage tank."

"But it takes a crew vote to elect a new coxswain."

"Yep. It does."

"You already voted?"

"Uh-huh. Unanimous. It's yours if you want it."

"Bunch of sneaky fuckers. I can't believe you've all managed to keep this quiet." He and Bryan went out into the yard where Marmite had found a patch of sun to lie in. The three other dogs surrounded him in a loose circle.

"See what I mean? Marm loves anything on four legs." Jed gave a short whistle. Marmite gave him a look that said 'you really want me to get up right now?' and took his own sweet time climbing to his feet. Bryan laughed. "Another one who has your measure. I swear he just rolled his eyes."

"He's bone idle. Aren't you?" Jed ruffled Marmite's fur. "I'll see you on auction day if there are no shouts before then. I'll have to think about the coxswain thing—talk to Jonty about it. It's a big commitment." He ushered Marmite into the van.

"There's no one better for the job, Jed." Bryan waved him off, leaving him with a lot to think about on the way home.

* * * *

Jonty knuckled his temples, sighing at how good it felt. He'd been hunched over his notepad all afternoon, making call after call, ensuring everything was ready for the auction. Talking to people he hardly knew wasn't easy and a tension headache had been building for a while. All he wanted to do was eat then snuggle beneath Jed's cozy duvet. He glanced at the clock. He'd run out of calls to make and Jed wasn't due to show up for another fifteen minutes. Only two other tables were occupied—it was the dead time between afternoon tea for walkers and the evening crowd—and Jonty was glad of the relative peace.

After a few minutes, Kelly wandered over to join Jonty at his table. "You've been busy this afternoon, that phone must be red hot by now."

"Yeah, I hope the rumors about the effects on your brain aren't true because I'm beyond saving by now." Jonty rubbed his neck. "I do have a rotten headache."

"You stressing out about the auction?" Kelly asked.

"A little." Jonty had so much information swirling around in his head he couldn't concentrate on anything anymore. "There's so much to think about and I don't want anything to go wrong. I want us to raise bucket-loads of money."

"And we will, but for now you need to relax. Making yourself ill isn't going to help. Are you waiting for Jed?"

"Yes, he's joining me for dinner so I hope you have something good on the menu." Jonty's stomach growled.

"You sound like Marmite."

"He only growls when he sees a cat. Or when someone stands between him and his bone. He doesn't mean anything by it, though."

"Well, I have a great chicken casserole tonight, with herb dumplings. Even though I say so myself, it tastes spectacular. It's one of Jed's favorites."

"Sounds fantastic. He should be here any minute. I hope he hasn't been delayed because I think my stomach is starting to eat itself." Jonty patted his flat belly. Right on cue, the door swung open letting in a blast of cold air. Jed pushed it closed then shrugged out of his waterproof.

"Raining again," he commented, not that it was necessary, because droplets of water shed from his coat onto the floor. "And it's cold enough to freeze the balls off a brass monkey." He marched across to where Jonty sat, gathered him into a hug then kissed him.

"Hey! Your face is cold," Jonty protested, pulling away.

"You see how quickly the bloom goes off a new relationship, Kelly. I'm already being rejected."

Kelly snorted. "I don't think so. You two are sweeter than my treacle tart." He pushed his chair back. "I'll go fetch some food. Mind if I join you while it's quiet?"

"Of course not," Jonty said. "Just bring extra big portions." He turned to Jed, "Where's Marmite?"

"Even the lure of Kelly's couldn't drag him away from a warm kitchen tonight, so I left him to it. That dog could snooze for England."

"He has the right idea." Jonty yawned. "Sorry, it's been a long day."

"Did you get all your calls done?"

"Almost. The only person I couldn't get hold of was the vicar and he's already delivered his contribution. I left a message. Everyone else knows what they're doing and when on the day. In theory."

"It will go fine, you'll see." Jed patted his knee. "You look a bit pale. Are you feeling okay?"

"Bit of a headache. Think I might need some stress relief later."

Jed's pupils dilated.

"Of course, you're probably tired too…"

"Nope. Full of beans, me. And I've got something to show you when we get home."

"What? Tell me!"

"It's a surprise."

"That's mean. Now I have to sit all through dinner wondering what you're up to." Jonty pouted. Kelly arrived with three bowls of aromatic casserole, so he couldn't sustain the expression. All three of them tucked in with gusto, Jonty moaning around every mouthful. "God, if I never get to eat another meal, I can die happy having tasted this."

"I hope there are seconds." Jed scraped out his bowl. Kelly grabbed it from him.

"Leave the pattern on it, will you? Yes, there's more. Anyone would think you two never get fed at all." He stomped back to the kitchen, returning with three refreshed bowls. This time Jonty ate a bit slower, savoring every scoop. By the time they'd finished, a few customers had begun to arrive so Kelly had to leave them and get back to business. Jonty leaned back in his chair.

"That was so good, but I'm ready to go home. You might have to carry me, though, I'm so full."

"I could sling you over my shoulder and carry you off to my boudoir if you like?" Jed leered.

"Boudoir is not a word I ever expected to hear coming out of your mouth, Jed Curnow. But the idea is tempting. Not sure my stomach would enjoy it on this occasion, though. Can we take a rain check?"

"We can." Jed fetched their coats from the hooks by the door. "From the sound of the wind out there, we'll probably have to hold each other up anyway."

Jonty shivered. "I hope the weather clears for the weekend."

"It's a stormy time of year. High tides, too. I wouldn't be surprised if we get a few call-outs over the next few days."

"Oh my God! What if you guys get a call on auction day? I hadn't thought of that."

"It won't matter, love. There are plenty of people to help who aren't on the crew."

"It won't be the same, though."

"Well, we'll just have to keep everything crossed that it doesn't happen, won't we?"

Chapter Fourteen

Jonty stared at Jed's creation in awe. "You made this for us? It's perfect!" Jed had set up the spanking bench in a corner of the bedroom. The scent of new leather filled Jonty's senses and he breathed deeply.

"It doesn't scare you, does it?" Jed stroked the padded top of the bench.

"No...well, maybe a little," Jonty said. "But it's a good scared. Anticipation, not dread, promise."

"Why don't you try it for size?"

Still fully clothed, Jonty felt awkward scrambling onto the bench. The cushioned top was comfortable and the sections supporting his limbs made him feel like he was floating. He could imagine himself naked, strapped down. His arse would be at Jed's mercy and that sent a thrill down his spine. Jed stroked his back.

"What do you think?"

"That I could sleep here, no problem. It's so comfortable."

Jed chuckled. "Good to know, but I don't think you'll be sleeping through what I have in mind." He patted Jonty's backside. "But your clothes are wet. I think we should share a hot shower."

Pressing his cheek against the leather, Jonty sighed. "Not sure I can move."

"You're draped there like one of those big cats you see in pictures – you know, where they're laid out along a tree limb with all four paws hanging down."

"I know what you mean," Jonty replied, giggling. He struggled up so that he sat, straddling the bench. "They always look so relaxed, but I think I'm more of a kitten than a predator."

"And I'm very glad of that." Jed lifted him from the bench then ushered him into the bathroom. "Let's get clean, and warm, so I can play with you." He set the water running.

"We seem to spend a lot of time getting cold and wet," Jonty said. "I prefer warm and sticky."

"I hope you're not thinking of moving from Cornwall to the Tropics." The twinkle in Jed's eye told Jonty he was being deliberately obtuse.

"Not right this minute." Jonty stripped off his clothes, dropping them where he stood. He gave his half-hard dick a few pulls. "Parts of me are in dire need of warmth." He took a single step closer to Jed. "A kiss might help." He tilted his head back, parted his lips and waited.

"You are a demanding brat, but I love you." Jed indulged him, capturing his mouth with unrestrained passion. He cupped the nape of Jonty's neck with one hand and his arse with the other. Jonty melted against him, humming his pleasure, but gradually became aware of an insistent beeping interrupting his tune. He pulled away. "You have got to be joking."

"It's my pager." Jed groped in his pocket. He glanced at the number before deactivating the annoying beep. "Well damn." He scrubbed a hand through his hair.

Jonty stepped beneath the shower. He began soaping himself, rubbing his hands over his body in blatant provocation. "Duty calls, love. Go! Be safe." He dropped the shower gel then bent to pick it up, turning so that Jed got a prime view of his rump.

"That bench is going to get a thorough testing in the morning. Go to bed, Jonty. I'll text you from the station once I know what the job is."

"Uh-huh." Jonty nipped his lower lip between his teeth while he jacked himself. "Love you loads." He listened to Jed muttering his frustration all the way down the stairs.

Though his climax was satisfying, it wasn't as much fun without Jed in the room. Jonty dried off then debated whether or not to get dressed. He was tempted to head down to the lifeboat station despite Jed telling him to go on to bed. He padded through to the bedroom where Marmite sat just inside the door.

"Missing him too, huh, boy?" Jonty ruffled the dog's fur. "Me too and he's only been gone ten minutes. What a pair we make." He checked his phone. There was a text from Jed, which just read *simple rescue, don't wait up xx*. "I don't know as any rescue is simple, Marm, but the wind has died down so I think we should get comfy, don't you? Need to dry my hair first or I'll look like a scarecrow come morning." Blow drying had to be shared with Marmite, who loved the warm air directed at him, so it took a lot longer than usual. By the time he was done, Jonty couldn't keep his eyes open. He tumbled into bed and Marmite clambered up next to him, taking up three-quarters of the space. "You're a space hog, Marm, and you're not allowed on the bed." Jonty didn't attempt to shift him. His warm presence was comforting, like a living breathing teddy bear, and in moments Jonty drifted off.

He stirred when the mattress dipped.

"Jed?"

"Who else were you expecting?"

Jonty pressed back against Jed's body. "Where's Marm?"

"He heard me come in. He's downstairs having a snack. He was on the bed, wasn't he?"

"I'm asserting my right to silence." Jonty wiggled in an attempt to get his arse closer to Jed's groin. "Mmm. You're hard."

"And you're half asleep." Jed stroked Jonty's flank. "So soft and smooth."

"There's lube under the pillow."

Jed soon pressed the tip of his cock to Jonty's fluttering hole. "Don't want to hurt you."

"You won't." Jonty pushed back. There was a slight pinch as Jed's cock pierced his body but the discomfort didn't last. Jed slung a leg over Jonty's thigh then settled into a slow, steady rhythm. He slipped an arm over Jonty's waist, reaching for his cock.

There was no need for words. Jonty let sensation take over as Jed's measured thrusts brought him to a shattering climax. Jed's release inside him was comfort and connection. He didn't pull free but instead pulled Jonty closer. Jonty drifted back to sleep still joined to his lover.

* * * *

"I had the most amazing dream last night," Jonty said, rolling over to lie on his stomach. He propped his chin in his hands. Jed, who had his head in a paperback thriller, smiled.

"You did? I can never remember my dreams, however good they were at the time." He put his bookmark in between the pages then closed the book. "Nightmares—they're a different story."

"This wasn't a nightmare."

"So tell me." Jed stroked Jonty's hair, wondering at how it slid through his fingers like silk.

"I dreamt I was sleeping and this big, handsome guy snuck into my bed and ravished me. I resisted of course but he was too strong so I had to give in."

"Sounds like you didn't put up *much* resistance."

"Well he was gorgeous—looked just like you in fact." Jonty giggled. "He had an enormous…"

"Take a shower, Jonty. You and I have an appointment with the spanking bench. Maybe you should make it a cold one because you won't be coming any time soon."

Jonty pouted. "You haven't told me about last night's rescue yet."

"That can wait. I have an urge to connect my hand with your arse."

"Help me with the kit?"

"Don't I always? You can say enema, you know. It's not a scary word." Jed leaned down to take a nip at Jonty's jutting lip. "Give me a shout when you're ready." Jed read a few more pages of his book while he waited. He wasn't sure how to express to Jonty how much he appreciated his trust. Jed would happily rub his back and whisper soothing words any time he needed them.

Once all the necessary bathroom procedures had been completed, Jed took a shower while Jonty relaxed. Once he was done, he pulled on a pair of black jeans but didn't bother with a shirt or shoes. Jonty, naked and glowing from his shower, lay on the bed, one hand wrapped around his dick.

"What exactly do you think you're doing?" Jed asked. He retrieved his favorite cock ring from a drawer.

"Um, nothing?"

"Hands off, sunshine." Jed fastened the leather ring around the base of Jonty's rigid shaft.

"But…"

"But nothing. Onto the bench."

"Now?"

Jed recognized procrastination when he saw it. He waited for Jonty to get comfortable with the idea of a morning spanking. "You have your safe word," he prompted.

Jonty scrambled out of bed before clambering onto the bench. "Ooh! It's cold." He wriggled into position. "And my dick is getting squished."

"Call it suffering for the cause." Jed ran his hand the length of Jonty's body. "I'm not going to tie you down. Not today. Consider yourself bound by my word."

Jonty pushed his arse against Jed's palm. "I like it when you touch me."

"That's good because I enjoy touching you. Very much." He stroked his finger through the cleft between Jonty's buttocks, teasing his hole. "Smooth and warm. You're beautiful, you know that?" Jed grabbed the lube. He coated two fingers before easing them inside Jonty's body. "Want you ready for me."

Jonty moaned and shifted as Jed prepped him. "Need you, Jed."

"You'll need me even more when your arse is warm and glowing." Jed cleaned his hands on a wad of tissues. "I think it's time we try out that paddle we chose together."

"I didn't even know it had arrived!" Jonty exclaimed. "Did you hide it from me?"

"It's been in plain sight in my underwear drawer."

"And why would I go in there?"

"Oh, I don't know." Jed fetched the paddle from the drawer. "You might like to ogle my shorts in secret for all I know."

"Hey! I'm not some boxer fetishist. I'm an artist."

Jed fell about laughing at the incongruous statement. "So what shade of pink should I aim for? Sunset rose, or maybe strawberry blush?" He gave Jonty's backside a gentle tap. The dimpled rubber coating on the paddle was thick with padding but even the light contact made Jonty jerk.

"Did you swallow a Dulux paint chart?" Jonty asked. "How about nice, normal pink?"

"I'm going to take it slow. Any time you feel uncomfortable, you know what to do."

"Not sure 'uncomfortable' is the right word to use there, Sir." Jonty grinned.

"You know what I mean, brat." Jed shook his head. Jonty's puppy eyes were even more appealing than those belonging to the real puppies at the farm. He began with gentle taps, watching for any sign that Jonty wasn't enjoying what he was doing. He built the force in increments, making sure to spread the blows across both cheeks. Jonty's whimpers grew louder as the color on his arse got darker, but he wasn't complaining. In fact Jed could hear "harder, damn it" at regular intervals. He didn't respond to those pleas. He would decide how much to deliver, no one else. When Jonty began wriggling in an attempt to get more friction to his cock, Jed laid the paddle aside. He pressed the palm of his hand to Jonty's skin, testing the heat.

"Perfect. Nice and warm. Still need me, love?"

Jonty responded with a string of expletives that ended in, "Get in me now!"

Jed unzipped his jeans, then obliged, grateful for his foresight in preparing Jonty earlier.

"Yesssss! Finally." Jonty shunted back, raising his backside a little. Jed grabbed his hips to hold him in place.

"Impatient little sod." He jacked his hips rapidly, enjoying the warmth each time he came into contact with Jonty's skin.

"Harder!" Jonty tried to reach beneath his body, presumably to get rid of the cock ring preventing his orgasm. Jed knocked his hand away, thrusting harder at the same time.

"Think you deserve to come, do you?" His own orgasm was imminent.

"Yes!" Jonty's scream could probably be heard across the water in South Wales.

"I'm not so sure." *God, but teasing him is fun.*

"Please, please, please, please, pleeeeeease!" Jonty twisted his head, begging with his eyes. Jed found it impossible to deny him.

"Up." He reached beneath Jonty's sweat-slicked body to release the snap on the cock ring.

"Oh!" Jonty wailed and came in one long spurt of release. His ecstatic noises ensured that Jed came right along with him, muscles straining as his orgasm tested his ability to stay standing. He gave Jonty's butt one final pat before pulling clear with care.

"Don't move, love. I'm going to fetch a flannel." When he got back from the bathroom, Jonty was still splayed across the spanking bench, limbs flopping.

"Think I'm stuck," he murmured. "Gonna have to stay here all day."

"But then I won't have the pleasure of watching you deal with a sore backside," Jed said, performing clean-up duty with a few gentle wipes. "Besides, if you don't get up, you'll end up attached by sperm superglue and I wouldn't recommend that."

"Oh, so much ickyness!" Jonty half-rolled, half-climbed from the bench. He collapsed onto the bed then lay still while Jed washed him down a bit.

"So, do you think we'll be doing that again?" Jed asked.

"Well, maybe not in the next hour," Jonty said. "But after that…definitely! It was so hot." He stuck a hand beneath his body, feeling his arse. "Ooh, different kind of hot!"

"And I have some gel to help cool it down. Roll over."

"So let me get this right. You spanked me to make it warm and now you're going to cool it down again."

"I spanked you because you need to be reminded who's in charge and because just the idea of it turns you on. It also pleases me—as does caring for you afterwards." Jed squeezed a dollop of glistening gel from a tube then spread it over Jonty's skin, eliciting several squeaks. "You'll ache for a while but you won't bruise."

"I wish I could see." Jonty craned his neck, trying to look.

"You get to feel instead." Jed sighed. "I wish I could stand here, petting your rear for the rest of the day, but the real world is calling."

"I wish you could too." Jonty turned over before sitting up. "I have to move the last few things out of Cliff House today because the new owners collect the keys this evening. Then the auction is tomorrow and I have to pick up the catalogues from the printer and check all the entries. There should be a courier arriving from London this morning with the last few pieces Shaw has purloined and the marquee is being put up." He made a grab for his clothes. "There's so much to do!"

Jed caught Jonty's wrist as he passed. He pulled his naked boyfriend into a hug. "And you need to calm down. Take a few deep breaths. You're going to eat a decent breakfast before you do anything."

"I don't have time." Jonty clung to him like a limpet.

"Yes, you do. In fact, I'll hide all your clothes unless you promise to eat."

"You want me to wander around naked?"

Jed cupped Jonty's arse with both hands. "Here, for me, always. No one else gets a show. There are worse punishments than a spanking, you know."

"Breakfast sounds like a great idea." Jonty batted his lashes.

"What am I going to do with you?"

"Whatever you want to," Jonty murmured.

Chapter Fifteen

Jonty hid in the lifeboat station toilets. He wasn't sure how long he could get away with it but his stomach was churning so he felt as if he had a reasonable excuse. That's what he was telling himself anyway. Beyond the safety of the locked door, chaos reigned, and he couldn't see how they were every going to be ready for the auction opening. Viewing was supposed to start at four and the first lot was due to go under the hammer at six. On the plus side, it had turned out to be a sunny day, warmer than usual for the time of year. The marquee people had arrived on time the previous day and had erected the huge tent with easy efficiency. Jonty had closed up Cliff House with no issues and no regrets. Jed had collected his easel, painting paraphernalia and a case of clothes in his van at lunchtime and, after one last look around the garden, Jonty had left and not looked back.

The negatives formed a somewhat longer list. He'd tossed and turned for most of the night, drifting into sleep only to wake again as auction-related worries snuck into his dreams. Rising before dawn, he had woken Jed when he'd tripped over his own shoes, which he'd left by the door the previous evening. Jed had plied him with tea, toast and kisses but then his pager had sounded and he'd disappeared toward the lifeboat station at a run, leaving Jonty and Marmite staring at each other in disbelief.

He still hadn't gotten back and it was past midday. Jonty wished he had a brown paper bag to breathe into. "Why did I think I could do this?" He put his head in his hands. "I couldn't save my family and now I can't even manage to run a charity event in their honor." Tears ran down his cheeks. A black nose appeared in the gap under the door. Marmite whined. "How did you get in here, Marm?" Jonty grabbed a handful of toilet roll then scrubbed his face dry. He blew his nose then flushed.

"Jonathon, are you in here? And why is there a woolly mammoth trying to get into that stall?"

"Shaw?" Pulling the lock back, Jonty stuck his head around the toilet door. Marmite shoved into him, knocking him back hard enough that he fell onto the toilet with Marmite's head in his lap.

"I see you have everything under control," Shaw said, a grin covering his bearded face.

Heat blossomed the full length of Jonty's body. He guessed his face resembled a ripe tomato. "Get off me, Marm." He struggled to his feet then half clambered half fell from the cubicle where Shaw enveloped him in a bear hug. "Hi, Shaw."

Shaw pushed him back, holding him at arm's length. "You've been crying. Jesus, Jonty, where's this man of yours and why isn't he looking after you?"

"He's at sea, on the lifeboat," Jonty snuffled. "And I don't need looking after."

Shaw snorted. "That's a matter of opinion. Who does the moose belong to?"

"He's not a moose, he's a Newfoundland. His name's Marmite and he belongs to Jed, or rather Jed belongs to him. In Marmite's mind that's the way it works, anyway."

"He's a very handsome boy." Marmite offered a paw to his admirer, which Shaw shook with due solemnity. "Got stuck with babysitting duty, eh, boy? He's hard work, isn't he?" Marmite gave a short bark of agreement.

"Hey! Stop talking about me, you two." Jonty stomped out of the bathroom in disgust. To his amazement, the chaos he'd left behind had been replaced by ordered calm. He gaped.

"Took me an hour to sort everything out," Shaw said. "Well, the missus actually. There are grown men quaking in fear out there."

"I'm not surprised. Alice is formidable. I'm glad you guys are here. I hate being in charge of anything."

"My pleasure. Have you any idea how much interest your little event has drummed up? When you sent me a picture of your contribution I almost wet myself."

"Way too much information, Shaw." Jonty giggled. "Let's have a walk around and check everything."

The paintings, photographs and wall hangings were all displayed in a training room, which had been commandeered for the event. Jonty's painting, which was to be the final lot of the evening, stood on an easel in the center of the room. It was a seascape depicting a violent storm but through a break in the angry clouds, a slither of light shone, illuminating the tips of the waves and the name of the yacht depicted battling the heaving ocean, *Caroline*.

Shaw planted himself in front of the painting. "This is a remarkable piece of work, Jonty. *New Hope* is an apt title."

Jonty stood next to him, Marmite leaning against his leg. "You know, every time I paint the sea, it's a kind of punishment. Self-flagellation. It brings back every nightmarish memory I have, but this one was different. Things have changed for me, Shaw. What happened wasn't my fault. I'm not owned by the sea anymore. Remembering still makes me sad—I don't think that will ever go away—but the guilt I've been carrying has gone."

"Because you have new focus. Jed. I can't wait to meet him."

"You will. If he ever gets back here."

"Do the locals have any idea of how much money this painting is going to make?"

Shrugging, Jonty walked over to the far wall. "Tell me what you think of this series." Four small watercolors hung in a straight line. Each depicted a local scene and the detail was exquisite. Shaw squinted at them.

"You did these." It wasn't a question. He examined each one in turn. "They are beautiful. Very different for you. I know someone…" He pulled out his phone, snapped a few shots then sent them into the ether. "Why didn't you tell me about these sooner?"

"I wasn't sure they'd be finished in time and I didn't know…well, I haven't worked in watercolors for a long time and you prefer oils."

Shaw shook his head. "How come you've never grown an ego?"

On the next wall were several atmospheric photographs, one of which Jonty loved and intended to bid on. It depicted a single, ancient oak, shrouded in mist. The photographer had captured the light perfectly, but what made the picture for Jonty was the fox in the corner of the picture, staring at the camera.

"I love this one. It came from one of your contacts, didn't it?"

"Another very talented young man. His name's Alistair—he's the partner of a friend of mine, Carey Hoffmann. Owns The Underground club, you may have heard of it?"

Jonty's face heated. "I have. Now I remember, *The Nightlife Exhibition*—it was all over the arts sections when it happened a couple of years back. Wow, we're lucky to have this picture. Will you bid on it for me, Shaw?"

"Sure. I'm acting as proxy for several other people. May as well add you to the list." He grinned. "Your boyfriend's piece excited a lot of interest. He's very gifted. Do you think you can use your powers of persuasion and convince him to create some more? Gallery space won't be a problem."

"You can ask him yourself," Jonty said. "Jed makes his own decisions." He nibbled his lower lip, thinking about how decisive Jed could be in the bedroom. "How about we go out to the marquee and check on things there?"

Shaw chuckled. "I really can't wait to meet this guy. Just his name gets you going, doesn't it?"

Marmite led the way outside, then got distracted by the barbecue where Saul and a couple of helpers were setting up. "Hey, Jonty, we're going to start cooking earlier than planned. Folks are hungry."

"Will you have enough sausages and burgers?"

"Not a problem. Arnie here" — he gestured to his redheaded assistant — "is on loan from the butcher's for the day. He can fetch more supplies when we need them."

"Sure can." Arnie grinned. "Mr. Settick will be along to help later as well."

"Sounds like you have everything in hand," Jonty said.

"Leave it to me." Saul was in his element. "First sausage is reserved for Marmite." Marmite flopped down beneath the drinks table.

"That's done it. He won't move now until he's got his treat," Jonty said.

"He'll be fine here with us. Me and the boys will keep an eye on him. Looks like the *Govenek* is on its way back too." Saul pointed out to sea.

Jonty whirled around and sure enough a bright orange blob in the distance headed toward the shore. His heart leapt. Jed was at the wheel of that boat and Jonty wished he had a rope he could attach to haul it in quicker. He wanted to run to the boat ramp but instead went into the marquee. One of Steve's colleagues, in uniform, stood by the entrance.

"Mr. Trelawn, very nice to meet you." He shook Jonty's hand. "Steve gave us all a description of you."

"Jonty, please. It's so good of you all to help out. I can't imagine there will be any trouble but..."

"A uniform or two around the place is a sensible preventative measure. I had a look at some of the work in here — there are some very talented people around, aren't there? Some of the jewelry could tempt an opportunist and Steve will kick our behinds if anything goes missing."

"Well, I appreciate you being here. I hope you'll have time to join in the fun later."

"There was a fight at the station for shifts, plenty of volunteers doing two hours each. A couple of the guys are walking around in civvies keeping an eye out too."

"I'm impressed," Shaw said. "Shaw Carney." He introduced himself. "Jonty's agent, down from London."

"Alice's husband?"

Puzzled, Shaw nodded.

"She's been keeping me supplied with refreshments. You're a lucky man."

"She always did have a thing for uniforms," Shaw muttered, heading inside the tent. Jonty followed him, laughing.

Inside chairs were set out in rows in front of a low platform and lectern. Around the edges of the marquee, two dozen tables held the various lots. Jonty had seen them all already but he was still amazed by the quality and creativity on display.

Shaw gaped. "You have some incredible work here." He wandered from table to table, taking the occasional photo. "This auction is going to cost me a fortune. You can bet Alice will have her mind set on a few of these."

"I love this quilt." Jonty fingered a patchwork creation in an array of blues and greens. "It would be perfect for my bed at the lighthouse."

"Lighthouse?"

"My new gallery and studio," Jonty explained. "Cliff House is sold and I needed somewhere to paint."

"I thought you had moved in with Jed?"

"Oh, I have. But he has one of the old fishermen's cottages on the quay. There's not enough light for a studio. The lighthouse is perfect. It's quiet and there's loads of room—I have a painting floor at the top, a kind of bedsit with a bathroom and mini kitchen in the middle and the gallery is on the ground floor. It's not quite ready yet, the auction has been taking up too much time, but you'll be invited to the grand opening in a few weeks."

"I'll be there—it sounds fantastic and if it means you paint more, I'm all for it." Shaw carried on perusing the lots and Jonty managed to stay calm. Inside the marquee he was protected from the hubbub outside. The door flap was pushed aside and Jed walked in, still wearing his sea gear.

"Jed!" Jonty ran to him. He jumped into Jed's arms, wrapping his legs around Jed's waist. He peppered his face with kisses. "You're all salty."

"And you have bloodshot eyes. Were you crying?"

"Who, me?"

"Don't avoid the question, Jonty." Jed put him on his feet.

"Um, how about I introduce you to Shaw?"

"Don't use me as a defense strategy," Shaw said, smiling. He shook Jed's hand. "Shaw Carney. It's a pleasure to finally meet you, Jed."

"Likewise."

"I'm going to leave you two together for a while and track down my wife. Jed, *someone* has been stressing out way too much over this whole event. He could use a break."

"Thanks, Shaw." Jed frowned. "You and I should have a long chat about this one later on."

"Hey! I'm right here." Jonty scowled. Shaw winked as he left.

"I'm going to dump my gear then we're going home for half an hour," Jed declared. "You can tell me about your morning. *All* about it."

Jonty sighed. "Yes, Sir." Just being near Jed helped him relax. He was more than ready for someone else to tell him what to do for a while.

* * * *

After a welcome hot shower, Jed wandered through to the bedroom where Jonty was sprawled on the bed. Marmite had stayed with Saul, far more enamored with grilling sausages than of his master.

"You're exhausted. You didn't sleep last night and you've no doubt been running around with your tail on fire all day. Your eyes tell me you've been crying, so spill it, Jonty. What's been going on?" Jed clambered onto the bed, patting the area between his legs. Jonty moved so that his back was pressed to Jed's chest. Jed wrapped both arms around Jonty's slender frame. "There's no escape. You're my prisoner, so you may as well confess."

"Or what?" Jonty asked. "Will you torture me or make me your sex slave?"

"Both ideas have potential." Jed slipped one hand down the front of Jonty's trousers, searching for his dick. "You've lost some weight. Your trousers are loose."

"Nng." Jonty drew his knees up. "Can't think when you're doing that."

Jed kept his fingers wrapped around Jonty's shaft, but stopped moving. "Talk to me."

"It all got a bit much for me, that's all. I hid in the toilets and had a cry. I don't want this to fail, Jed. I owe it to my parents, to Evie, to you and the crew of the *Govenek*. I was helpless that day. I don't want to feel the same way ever again."

"You don't owe anyone anything," Jed chided. "You put far too much pressure on yourself."

"It's different when you're here. I feel more grounded. Safe."

"I'm sorry I had to go this morning, it was bad timing." Jed undid Jonty's jeans in order to gain better access to his burgeoning erection.

"What happened?" Jonty's words came out at a higher pitch than usual.

"Two kids out walking with their dog on the beach further along the coast didn't take notice of the tide times and got themselves cut off. We sent the small dinghy in to get them. They were scared, but unharmed." Jonty's cock was warm in his hand. He brushed his thumb over the tip.

Jonty moaned. "You've had a much more stressful day than I have. Oh God, don't stop!"

"I've got you." Jed jacked Jonty's shaft until he tensed. "You want to come?"

"Yes! Yes, please."

Pressing his nail into Jonty's slit, Jed squeezed hard. Jonty yelled then came in a gush, hands fisting the bed covers.

"Remember to breathe, sweetheart." Jed stroked Jonty through the aftershocks of his orgasm. Jonty was limp and pliable, exactly how Jed has intended. "Feeling better?"

"Uh-huh. So relaxed."

"My work here is done."

"What about you?" Jonty wriggled, attempting to turn over, but Jed held him in place.

"I'm good. That was for you. I think you needed it."

"Need *you*," Jonty murmured.

"You've got me. Always."

"We have to go back to the real world, don't we?"

"This is your big day, Jonty. All your hard work will pay off and everything is going to go perfectly."

"I'm going to clean up a bit. Then I'll be ready." Jonty giggled. "It makes a change for me to be dressed while you're bare-arsed naked. I like it."

"Don't be getting ideas, sunshine." Jed dressed then followed Jonty to the bathroom and, between kisses, they made themselves respectable. Jed checked his watch. "Viewing starts in ten minutes. We should be there to answer questions."

"Can I stand behind you, while *you* answer them?" Jonty tied his hair back though some strands floated free straight away. Jed tucked them behind Jonty's ear.

"I don't think that will work. How about we try this... If it gets too much for you, put your safe word into a sentence and I'll get you somewhere quiet quicker than Marm scarfs his breakfast."

"We can do that?"

"We can do anything we want."

"I love you. It's a brilliant idea, and a good job we settled on starfish rather than sea cow for my safe word."

"See, I knew you wanted me for my mind, not my body."

Jonty bounced down the stairs. "I wouldn't go that far. All those yummy muscles have some appeal."

"Yummy?" Jed went after him. "I'm not yummy!"

Jonty hared out of the house with Jed hot on his heels. They were both laughing. Jed soon caught up. He grabbed Jonty around the waist, swinging him in a circle, before pulling him into a kiss. When he was done, he put Jonty back on his feet.

"*You* are trouble."

"Can I be *in* trouble instead?" Jonty asked, running his tongue over his lower lip in blatant provocation.

"I don't want Steve to arrest me," Jed replied. "You can be in trouble when we get home tonight." They reached the lifeboat station and Jed took a bit more notice of his surroundings. A huge queue of people snaked along the quay. He caught Steve's eye and waved him over. "What's going on?"

"Jonty's publicity drive worked."

"I don't understand?" Jonty, wide-eyed, joined them.

"The auction has been on local radio and TV. There are posters up along most of the north coast of Cornwall and some arts program on BBC4 did a bit of promo. There are people here from all over the country, even some from abroad. We're having to limit numbers in the tent and lifeboat station, hence the line."

"Where are they all parking?" Jed asked.

"Simon Argawl rang me to say he's had to open up three more fields for parking. His cows aren't that impressed and he reckons he'll need the tractor to haul some of the cars out later but he's charging everyone a couple of quid, which he'll donate to the cause. He's also sold out of cheese, yogurt and eggs, so he's a happy man."

Jed caught Jonty backing away, an expression close to panic on his face. He grabbed his hand. "Where do you think you're going?"

"Home? Somewhere…anywhere."

"Take a few deep breaths, love. I'm right here."

"Sorry. Sorry." Jonty's hunched shoulders relaxed. "This is good, right?"

"It's amazing. You're going to raise a lot of money."

"We," Jonty corrected him. "We are going to do that. All of us."

"Exactly. There are a lot of people here supporting you. Are you going to be okay?"

"Just don't leave me." Jonty squeezed his hand.

"Never."

"Hey, Jed!" Jed glanced in the direction of the shout to find Kelly walking toward them. "Isn't this fantastic?" He gestured at the crowds. "Thank God for the WI. Think they've poured about eight hundred cups of tea and dished up half a ton of sponge so far. Saul's barbecued enough meat to feed a small army and the Crusty Crab has people sitting out in the street on borrowed garden chairs."

"We do seem to have drawn a crowd." Jed kept a protective arm around Jonty's shoulders.

"The TV people want to speak to Jonty. They're in the lifeboat station if you want to make a run for it. I'll cover for you."

"No, I'll talk to them. It's the least I can do," Jonty said, and to Jed's surprise he was pulled in the direction of the station. Jonty seemed to have gained a new personality. He chatted to people he recognized as they passed, shook hands with visitors who recognized him, petted dogs and cooed over babies.

"What's gotten into you?" Jed asked, amazed at the transformation.

"It's repressed panic." Jonty's grin was a little manic.

"Okay then."

Jonty began his interview with the film crew talking like he'd imbibed several cans of Red Bull but when they mentioned his parents, he froze. "Starfish. I think starfish are beautiful." The interviewer looked confused but Jed stepped in.

"Mr. Trelawn needs to take a break now. He hasn't eaten and he's a bit shaky." He waved Kennick over. "Kennick was the coxswain of the lifeboat that night. He can fill you in on the official record of what happened." Kennick nodded his understanding and Jed guided Jonty outside to the sea wall. "Take a few deep breaths, love."

Jonty let out a shuddering sob. "I'm so sorry. I thought I could do it, I really did. But then she asked about Mum and Dad and a wave crashed over me just like on that night. I could see Dad, on the floor of the cabin, Mum crushed under the mast. Evie taking her last breath in my arms. Oh God."

"And you remembered what to do. You used your safe word." Jed walked him away from the crowds, never letting go of his hand. "No more interviews, Jonty. No more trying to be someone you're not. There's nothing wrong with being shy and no one in this village is ever going to make you do something you don't want to do. People here love you. They'll form a wall in front of you if they have to."

"I'll be okay. I just need a minute… I don't like crowds."

"Not that keen myself." Jed pulled Jonty into a hug. "Brisk sea breeze will do us both good."

"I don't know what I'd do without you, Jed."

"You did just fine before I came along."

"No, I didn't. I realize that now. I was barely functioning, then you and Marmite came into my life and the mist cleared. You know that freshness that envelopes everything after a rainstorm? That's the feeling you gave me."

"Very glad to be of service." Tears welled in Jed's eyes. He fumbled in his pocket. "I was going to wait until later before I gave you this, but I think the time is right."

"What is it?"

Jed handed over a slim silver chain with a delicate clasp. Hanging from it was a carved wooden pendant. "It's my take on a Cornish love ring."

The flat disc of ebony had an inscription around the edge, delicately carved and set with silver. Jonty read it out. "*Un bysow dhe dhysquedhes agan kerensa*. I probably said that all wrong. What does it mean?"

"It translates as 'One ring to show our love'," Jed replied. "During the twelfth century, the Cornish knight Tristan defeated the Irish knight Morholt to bring the fair Iseult home for his uncle, King Mark, to marry. On the journey back to Cornwall, after ingesting a love potion, Tristan and Iseult fell madly in love. Their complete devotion to each other is symbolized by the Cornish love ring. One day I'd like to give you a ring for your finger, but for now I hope you'll wear this for me."

"It's beautiful. The carving in the center is stunning." The wood was pierced in an intricate knot work design.

"It stands for the continuity of life."

"It's perfect. Will you put it on for me?"

Jed fastened the chain around Jonty's neck. The pendant lay flat against his chest, a dark contrast with his pale skin. "You know this means you're mine now."

"I always was. You did so much more than save me from the sea, Jed. You saved me from myself."

Jed kissed him, long and slow, while the remains of the sun dipped below the horizon. "Romantic as this is, if we don't move our arses we're going to miss the auction — and I'm the auctioneer, so that wouldn't be good."

"Shaw will be having kittens too, wondering where I am. He's done a lot to support the auction. I don't want to let him down."

They headed back to the tent at a run but people were still filing inside. Jed took his place on the rostrum while Jonty took a seat at the back next to Shaw. Jed gave him a wave from up front. He tapped the microphone and the crowd quietened but the hum of excitement was still evident.

"Good evening, ladies and gentlemen." Jed surveyed the packed marquee and the line of volunteers ready to take phone bids. "If everyone is ready, we'll begin."

From his position in the back corner of the tent, Jonty could just see Jed through the crowd. He had Shaw to his right and to his left a woman he didn't know whose ample bosom blocked his view of the rest of the row. He was amazed at the number of people present and very proud of Jed, completely at ease on the rostrum. Shaw's copy of the catalogue was covered in his illegible scrawl. Every lot seemed to have a note against it.

"How many lots are you bidding on?" Jonty whispered. There were almost two hundred items up for auction.

"Thirty or so." Shaw kept his eyes on Jed. "Some for me. Some for clients."

There was a round of applause as Jed concluded the first item, a stunning glass vase shot through with gold leaf, which fetched far more than its estimate. There was a disturbance in the row and Jonty realized that Marmite was barging his way along. He flopped down at Jonty's feet — well, on his feet — his solid weight oddly comforting. Jonty scratched his ears and listened as the bidding escalated on a circular mirror with a carved cherry wood surround.

Item after item went under the hammer and Jonty was delighted at the prices everything was fetching. Shaw bid on a small bronze of a rearing horse, then on a silver pendant set with a polished fossil. He won both.

"That's Alice's birthday present sorted. Her hints were about as subtle as an elephant trampling a daisy."

Jonty let the bidding wash over him. It took a while to get through all the lots in the tent and they all had to be sold before the artwork from the training room could be brought in, one item at a time. Once the tables around the marquee were cleared, Jed announced a break.

"I don't know about everyone else, but I need a drink. Please take advantage of the refreshments on offer outside and we'll reconvene in twenty minutes." The noise level rose as people left their seats, heading for the various offerings of food and drink. Jonty stayed put, as did Marmite, waiting for Jed to make his way over. Shaw excused himself then went to find his wife, muttering something about making sure she wasn't bidding against him. Jed dropped into the seat next to Jonty.

"It's going well, isn't it?"

"It sure is! I can't believe the prices we're achieving. Your seabird made over five hundred pounds."

"Shaw bought it, didn't he?"

"Which means he knows he can get even more for it in his gallery — he's not daft."

"He asked me about supplying him with more work. I think it might be fun."

"You could work on those at the lighthouse while I paint, and keep the workshop for furniture," Jonty suggested.

"And how much work would either of us get done then?"

"Are you saying I'm a distraction?" Jonty blinked, affecting innocence.

"The fact that you're even asking the question suggests you know the answer already, young man."

"Who me?"

"Uh-huh. How about we get a drink and a snack before the rest of the auction?"

"If you can get Marmite to shift, I'd love that."

"Watch this… Sausages, Marm." Marmite leapt to his feet, all four paws leaving the ground. His tongue lolled. "See. Easy."

Jonty allowed Jed to tow him to the back of the barbecue area, where he persuaded Saul to part with two hotdogs with the works and two sausages without buns for Marmite. He grabbed two Cokes from a cooler under Saul's table then they joined several other people who'd opted to sit on the harbor wall. Two bites and Marmite's sausages were gone. He lay down, looking at Jed and Jonty with mournful eyes as they ate their food.

"This is so good," Jonty said between mouthfuls. "I didn't realize how hungry I was."

"And auctioneering is thirsty work." Jed downed his drink in a few long swallows. "How are you doing?"

Jonty fiddled with his pendant. "I'm fine when the attention isn't on me, and it's kind of fun watching Shaw bid."

"There are a lot of phone bidders too."

"Half of Shaw's client list, I suspect."

Jed stood. He massaged his arse.

"I could do that for you," Jonty offered.

"If we didn't have to get back inside, I'd take you up on the offer."

Jonty's fingers itched to touch. He would much rather head home to bed than go back to the marquee but he consoled himself with the fact that the day was almost over.

"I'm proud of you, you know." Jed took Jonty's hand and gave his fingers a squeeze. "You've achieved miracles here today. The village has pulled together to support you in a way I've never seen before."

"I didn't do much."

"Remind me to spank you later—for not taking credit when it's due." Jed gave Jonty's arse a pat.

"Yes, Sir." They had reached the tent. Jonty let go of Jed's hand with some reluctance, but he couldn't help smiling. Shaw was saving his seat and this time Alice was with him. Jonty joined them while Jed walked down the aisle to take his place on the rostrum.

"Hi, Alice," Jonty said. "Come to keep this one under control?" He nudged Shaw.

"He's like a pig in muck, Jonty love. In his element. But he forked out for a nice hotel with a four-poster and a spa bath, so I can't complain, and I've had so much fun helping out today. You have lovely friends and neighbors."

"I suppose I do. I hadn't taken notice before I started organizing all this. I've been sleepwalking through life for a long time."

"But now you've found a man who has woken you up, right?" Alice nodded in Jed's direction. "You're a lucky boy. That is one prime piece of real estate."

"Alice!" Jonty's face heated, even though he agreed.

"Quiet, you two," Shaw hushed them. "Jed's getting started again."

Alice rolled her eyes but settled back in her seat. Jonty fixed his eyes on Jed, not really listening to the bidding going on around him. Tracking Jed's motions and expressions was much more entertaining. Jonty was quite content to daydream about new adventures in the bedroom — all the possibilities that a relationship with Jed would bring. He pictured himself as a flower bud that had been tightly closed in self-protection against the frost. Jed's warmth had enticed him to unfurl, bit by bit, and now he wanted his petals warmed by the sun. He laughed at his own imagination, earning a nudge from Shaw, but an image formed in his mind that he thought might become a painting.

"Your series is up next," Shaw whispered.

"An unusual series of exquisite watercolors by award-winning local artist Jonathon Trelawn." Jed introduced the set with a grin. "Outside his usual medium, highly desirable and certain to command a good price. Can I start the bidding at one thousand pounds?" Several paddles waved. Three volunteers indicated they were dealing with telephone bidders. The offers rose fast and Jonty ducked his head, trying to avoid attention. Shaw hadn't raised his paddle yet and the series had already passed the catalogue estimate of ten thousand pounds. Jonty held his breath. Jed announced a bid of thirty thousand. He got to 'going twice' then Shaw flicked his paddle, raising the bids again. After a final flurry, Shaw won the lot at an astonishing fifty thousand pounds. Jonty gaped at him but Shaw just shrugged.

"My buyer was prepared to pay more. He got a bargain. He'll be insuring them for double that — not that he'd sell. He's an avid collector of your work. Bit of a fanatic actually. If he didn't live abroad, I'd be worried he might try to collect you too."

Jonty gulped. "You know some...eccentric people." He watched as the next picture was placed on the easel at the front of the room. It was the photograph he coveted and had asked Shaw to bid on. The photograph made a great price but within the limit Jonty had set, so he was delighted. If he and Jed ever made it to London they would have to venture to The Underground to meet the talented photographer. *As well as enjoy the facilities.* That thought set him to daydreaming again and wishing he had a catalogue to put in his lap. He tried some deflating thoughts but nothing worked until he realized that it was time for the final lot of the night—his oil of the *Caroline*.

Seeing the painting on the stand brought mixed emotions. He knew it was good, but it brought with it the sting of salt water against his skin, the throbbing ache of a broken arm and the searing pain of loss. Blood pounded in his ears. The bidding raced up but it was Shaw who eventually held out, offering what seemed to Jonty like a ridiculous amount of money. Spontaneous applause broke out. Jonty looked for somewhere to hide but he was hemmed in. He managed a tentative smile and a nod, then Jed began to bring proceedings to a close.

"I want to thank everyone here for their support today. Without all of you, this fundraising effort would not have been possible. There are local bands playing and more food and drink on offer on the quay tonight, so please enjoy yourselves. We'll be announcing a rough total raised at midnight, once we've had a chance to warm up the abacus. Good night!"

Cheering and more applause were followed by a general stampede toward the exit, while successful bidders went to settle up and collect their items. Jonty remained in his seat, accepting pats on the back and congratulations with as good grace as he could manage. Music started up from the direction of the stage outside.

"I'm off to arrange money transfers," Shaw said. "See you outside later." He and Alice left Jonty alone in the back row. He was trembling, suddenly cold as if overtaken by the onset of a fever. His vision blurred. Then he was scooped into Jed's arms.

"You look shattered, love." Jed held him close.

"It has been quite a day," Jonty murmured.

"I can't wait to get you home, tucked under the duvet with a mug of hot chocolate laced with brandy."

"That sounds so good." Jonty already felt better. "But I want to enjoy the last couple of hours."

"Are you sure? We could sneak away."

"No. Lots of people have put a huge amount of effort into this for me and I haven't even had a chance to talk to some of them yet. I'm not going to hide when they're still working away."

Jed put a finger beneath Jonty's chin, tilting his head back. Jonty parted his lips, inviting a kiss. Jed began with a gentle touch, flicking his tongue inside Jonty's mouth. He cupped his face then pressed his claim with a kiss that made Jonty's knees buckle. As they separated, Jonty ran his tongue over his lips, tasting mint. "Yum." Jed stroked his cheek.

"I'm giving you stubble burn."

"Don't care." Jonty grinned. "Kissing you is way better than caffeine as a stimulant. Let's go find Steve. I want to know how his security team are getting on."

Feeling energized, he pulled Jed outside, stopping to take in the scene. In the water, the lifeboat floated with all its lights on. Some of the crew were demonstrating a night rescue and a crowd of children were watching from the harbor wall. Beth and the landlord of the Crusty Crab had opened the beer tent and seemed to be doing a roaring trade, as were the barbecues. Saul had delegated cooking duties and was parked on a hay bale outside the beer tent sipping a pint. He gave them a cheerful toast.

"Bloody brilliant day, lads."

Jed chuckled. "That about sums it up, Saul."

The WI had run out of baked goods but were doling out mugs of tea and coffee. Kelly had been pressed into service and was reveling in the attention.

"Jed, Jonty! I blame you two for my dish pan hands. I've never done so much washing up in my life." He held up his hands, clad in a pair of bright yellow Marigolds.

"They suit you, mate. You could start a new fashion trend," Jed shouted, receiving a less polite form of wave in return, which earned Kelly a clip round the ear from the octogenarian supervising him.

A big crowd was in front of the stage dancing to a local band. The singer was belting out popular covers in an attempt to be heard over the audience, which was singing along. Jonty lost count of the number of people who spoke to him. They all seemed to know him but though some were familiar, the majority were strangers to him.

"I'm going to have to keep a close eye on you," Jed remarked. "I see covetous glances everywhere."

"It's just your imagination." Jonty laughed. "Are you looking for an excuse to put me on a lead?"

"In a cage, maybe," Jed retorted, making Jonty's dick twitch.

"Perhaps we *should* go home." A comfortable bed and Jed's cock filling his arse would make the perfect combination after a long, stressful day. Jed just laughed then steered him into the lifeboat station.

To Jonty's relief it was a bit quieter inside. The training room that had been an impromptu gallery was now accounting central. Steve, keeping a watchful eye on proceedings, stood in one corner. Two tables held laptops, pen, paper and Tupperware boxes full of cash. Behind them, Aileen from the post office and Cora, who was a bank teller in Newquay, counted, recounted and checked every penny. Neither of them looked up.

Steve ambled over. "Marmite's in the kitchen if you were wondering where he'd disappeared to," he said. "I'm guarding the cash."

"There appears to be a lot of it," Jed noted.

"Sure is. The auction alone raised almost a quarter of a million, thanks to Jonty. The ladies are counting the takings from food and drink sales, collection buckets et cetera. Even the TV crew that were here earlier had a whip round before they went."

"That's fantastic." Jonty couldn't believe the amount. "Did you get to bid on anything?"

"I won a pendant for Rose," Steve said. "She'll be surprised."

"That's wonderful."

"Shaw gave me the photograph you bought so I put it in my locker. Do you want to take it now?"

"No, I'll pick it up tomorrow," Jonty said. "It will be safe enough in there." He nudged Jed. "Can we get a cup of tea in the kitchen, check on Marmite?"

"A couple of the lads are in there," Steve offered. "The ones that don't do crowds very well—Callum and Bryan."

"Sure. I wouldn't mind a brew if there's one going. Those two are bound to have a pot on the go." Jed smacked his lips together.

"You and your tea. I think the world would end if we ever ran out of the stuff." Jonty headed for the kitchen. When he pushed the door open he found Callum and Bryan at the table, teapot between them, both holding steaming mugs and looking guilty. On his usual blanket in the corner, Marmite opened one eye. His ears twitched when he spied Jed but he didn't move. Between his front paws lay a ball of white fluff.

"Marmite's found himself a new toy," Jonty said, wondering why Jed was grinning like a lunatic. "Oh my God, it's moving!" A tiny nose, bright eyes and miniature paws became apparent. Jonty dropped to his knees in front of Marmite. He lifted the fluff ball free, cradling it in his hands. "It's a puppy!"

"He's observant, isn't he?" Callum said. "Must be the artist in him." He poured two more mugs of tea, ignoring Jonty's glare.

"I think it's the same one I looked after a while back. He had a black spot as well. He's a bit bigger now, though." Jonty cuddled the pup to his chest. "What's he doing here?"

"Waiting for his new master," Callum said.

"Jed, what's going on?" Jonty didn't want to put the puppy down in case someone tried to take him.

"You'd better start thinking about a name," Jed suggested.

"I don't understand." Realization gradually dawned as Jonty's tired brain processed Jed's words. "You mean he's mine?"

"Or you're his." Jed sipped his tea. "I think that's more likely."

Jonty didn't know what to say. He wanted to cry he was so happy. He took the chair next to Jed, laying the pup in his lap where it promptly went back to sleep. "I'm going to call him Doodle," he announced. Marmite came and sat by him, nosing at the little white bundle. "He's fine, Marmite. We have to share the cuddles, okay?" Marmite huffed.

"Doodle's a perfect name." Jed stroked the puppy's head with one finger. "Something makes me think you'd already decided."

"I kind of hoped…" Jonty admitted. "Thank you, Jed. Thank you so much!" He wanted to hug and kiss him but decided restraint was needed in front of Callum and Bryan—though the two men had wide grins and shining eyes. "I can't believe he's really mine." The puppy whimpered then burrowed against his sweater. "I can't wait to take him home."

"He's had his inoculations," Callum said. "And you're welcome to bring him to visit his mum any time. We're keeping one of his sisters at the farm as well. The rest of the litter all have homes now."

Jonty nodded. "I'd love that." For a while he sat, enjoying the quiet while the others chatted. Every now and again, Doodle stirred, snuffled then went back to sleep. His warmth soaked through to Jonty's skin. When it got close to midnight, Jed pushed his chair back.

"Come on. It's time for the big announcement."

Jonty didn't want to leave Doodle but he laid him back on the blanket with Marmite. Callum offered to stay and keep an eye on them. "It's your big moment, Jonty. You can't miss it," Callum said.

"Last thing to do, then we can all go home." Jed grabbed his hand. "Come and take your bow."

They made their way outside, then onto the stage. Everyone who was still standing gathered around. Someone handed Jed a slip of paper. He tapped the microphone, testing it. "It has been an incredible day. Those of us who man the lifeboat can't express how grateful we are for this show of support. And now, to announce the provisional total raised, here is the man behind today's event, Jonathon Trelawn."

Jonty had to wait a good two minutes before the cheering died down. "I'm no good at speaking," he said, "so I'm just going to read this number out and add my thanks to everyone who helped pull all this together. This is my way of thanking the amazing lifeboat crew that saved my life, and remembering my family." Jed handed him the slip. He looked at the handwritten figure in amazement. "The total raised today has been…two hundred and fifty-one thousand pounds and eighty-two pence!" His last words were drowned out by the cheering. The paper fell from his fingers as he threw himself into Jed's arms. "We did it!"

"Your family would be incredibly proud." Jed hugged him. "It's a fitting tribute."

"I wish they were here."

"The best you can do is live the life they would have wanted for you."

Jonty rested his head on Jed's shoulder. For the first time he could look forward to the future without guilt.

The sadness would never fade, but happiness now held a much bigger place in his heart.

Epilogue

Jonty's lips parted. He panted, riding Jed's cock with determined concentration. His body rolled from his hips, through his abs, to his chest. He flung his head back, focused on giving Jed as much pleasure as he could. His bound hands bumped the top of his arse as he moved, an arse still sore from the spanking Jed had delivered that morning. Jonty relished the ache, which let him feel Jed's presence even when they were apart. It made him look forward to moments like this when they could be alone and joined in the most intimate way possible. The deep love he felt came close to overwhelming him at times.

He glanced at his rigid shaft, wound with black cord that constricted the point just below the head as well as the base of his balls. There was no way he would be able to come unless Jed released him and that sent a thrill the length of his spine — almost as good as an orgasm. *Almost.*

"Will you let me come, Jed?" Jonty gasped out the words. He wished he could run a finger through the sheen of perspiration coating Jed's muscular chest. Jed squeezed his hips.

"Well, let's see. Did you let Doodle sleep on the bed again last night?"

"Uh…" It was impossible to answer questions when Jed was so deep inside him.

"And because Doodle was there, did Marmite want to join him?"

"I… Please, Jed!"

"And whose side of the bed do they always try to occupy?"

"Yours!" Jonty screamed as Jed nailed his prostate yet again.

"So do you think you deserve to come?"

"How are you still talking?" Jonty asked. Jed held him so just the tip of his cock remained inside Jonty's body. Jonty stared at the view from the lighthouse through the colored panes of the treasured stained-glass panel that had been his gift to Jed. It was getting late and the spectacular sunset had given way to midnight velvet shot with pinpricks of starlight. It was breathtaking.

"Because I live to torment you, love."

Jonty pushed against Jed's resistant hold. Jed let him sink down until he rested on his thighs, Jed's cock fully seated inside him. He wiggled his arse in an attempt to get Jed even deeper. "Oh…that's so good." He squeezed his inner muscles and Jed's eyes widened. Jonty focused every atom of his being on Jed's pleasure rather than his own. Jed growled and bucked beneath him and Jonty could sense he was close from the tension in his muscles.

"Don't stop…"

From Jed it was a sacrifice of control that Jonty rarely witnessed. He loved that he could bring his strong, handsome partner to such a point where he was at Jonty's mercy. He rolled his hips, increasing the speed of his rise and fall. Jed's grasp tightened, he sucked in his breath, then came in a rush of heat. Jonty gave a shout of triumph, relishing Jed's pleasure.

"You just earned yourself a reward." Jed released the bindings around Jonty's cock before taking it in hand. He applied pressure in the all the right places, making Jonty squirm and gasp. With Jed still inside him, Jonty came, shouting Jed's name. Jed untied his hands and finally he could get them onto Jed's skin. He touched every inch he could reach while his orgasm continued to race through him, spattering Jed's chest with his release.

"Wow! Oh, wow." Jonty sagged, lying against Jed's chest. "I don't think I'm ever going to be able to move again."

Jed stroked his back. "We don't have to, for a while." He pulled the blue and green patchwork cover over them. "It was worth the effort of hauling a new bed up here, wasn't it?"

Jonty giggled, recalling the day he had supervised Jed and Kelly as they'd heaved parts of the bed up the spiral staircase. "One time I got to be in charge. I thought I was going to be scraping bits of you and Kelly off the stairwell."

"And why do you find that funny?"

"I don't." Jonty shook his head. "Not me. Nope."

"Liar." Jed rolled them over so Jonty was beneath him. "Another punishment to add to the list." He licked him, making Jonty laugh.

"Stop! That tickles." He loved having Jed's weight on him, holding him down. It made him feel safe. He wrapped a leg around Jed's thigh. "Love you."

"Love you too." Jed sighed. "We should get back, I suppose." He moved to one side, reaching for the wipes next to the bed. Jonty took them from him, using a few to clean Jed's chest. "The dogs will need a quick walk before bed."

"Mmm. Bed."

"You're insatiable!"

"No, just inspired by your gorgeous body."

Jed chuckled. "In that case, it *is* time to go."

Facilities at the lighthouse were basic but good enough for a quick clean-up. The heat of a summer's day had dissipated but Jonty didn't need more clothing than shorts and a T-shirt. He slipped his feet into his sandals then waited for Jed to finish dressing.

"I love it here, but home is wonderful too. We're so lucky to have two places to call our own."

"Home is wherever you are," Jed replied. "But you're right — we are lucky. Lucky we found each other."

Jonty headed down the stairs to the next level. The work on the lighthouse was complete and he was looking forward to opening his gallery in a few days. The studio had perfect light and he was keeping Shaw very happy with his productivity as a result. It was a special place that he and Jed could enjoy without interruptions while they explored each other.

They walked back to the cottage hand in hand. Fresh, clean air filled Jonty's lungs and he wanted to laugh out loud. They passed Kelly's Place, which was brightly lit, music coming from the open door and windows. On the quay, fishermen cast their lines watched by lingering strollers. A cat sat on a wall, surveying its territory with flashing green eyes. Jonty breathed in the atmosphere, which had all the comfort of familiarity, and listened to the rush of the sea across shingle.

Inside the cottage, Doodle threw himself at them with carefree abandon while Marmite gave a more measured greeting.

"I'll make hot chocolate if you take them out for a few minutes," Jonty offered.

Once Jed and the dogs had disappeared, he put a pan of milk on the stove to heat. Fingering the pendant around his neck he gazed at the photograph on the mantel—it pictured an ancient oak silhouetted against a moonlit sky and in the corner, a fox had snuck into the image. He laughed, remembering the night of the auction when Jed had surprised him with the gift of the patchwork quilt he'd fallen in love with. Jed had bought it for him by getting the vicar to bid on his behalf.

"Sneaky, wonderful man." He broke some chocolate into the heating milk, wondering how his life could get any better. Jed and the dogs hustled back inside. Marmite picked up his plush lobster then settled into his bed in front of the Aga. Doodle tore around the kitchen for a few minutes until Jonty scooped him up for a cuddle.

"I never get tired of watching Marmite with Doodle's lead in his mouth. He takes such good care of the little guy," Jed commented.

"Just like you take care of me," Jonty said. "He has a great role model. Though Marm is much more laid-back than you are."

"And Doodle is naughtier than you." Jed accepted a mug of hot chocolate and a kiss. "Though you have your moments."

"I don't know what you mean." Jonty feigned innocence.

"Oh, I think you do." Jed took his mug away then put it and his own on the table. He laid his pager next to it. "I'm off duty for the next forty-eight hours and it's Saturday tomorrow, so no work."

"Is the coxswain going to get all masterful with me?" Jonty walked into Jed's arms.

"I might."

"Did you know the word literally means boat servant? I looked it up."

"Your point is?" Jed massaged Jonty's cock through his trousers.

"No point!" Jonty squeaked. "I like you being in charge."

"And I'm happy you didn't mind me accepting the role."

"I still worry," Jonty admitted. "But separating you from the sea would make you unhappy and then *I'd* be unhappy."

"And we can't have that." Jed picked him up and Jonty wrapped his legs around Jed's waist. He carried him up the stairs to their bedroom, laying him on the bed with gentle care. "How about we engage in a bit of mutual happiness?"

"Yes please." The distant crash of waves provided the perfect soundtrack as Jed stripped him bare. Naked beneath Jed's cornflower blue gaze, Jonty smiled. "I'm all yours."

Want to see more from this author? Here's a taster for you to enjoy!

Testing Lysander
L.M. Somerton

Excerpt

"You need your head read, young man. You treat photography like an extreme sport."

"And your bedside manner needs some work, Doc." Brock winced and gritted his teeth as another needle punctured his flesh.

"Would you rather I patted your head and gave you a sugar lump?"

"Is that what you did in the army?" Brock often thought that his doctor forgot he was now dealing with delicate civilians.

"Most squaddies would run away screaming at the sight of a needle if it didn't mean disciplinary action. I often wish the same principles could be applied to my patients here."

Brock squirmed. "I don't remember vaccinations ever being this painful and I've had enough of them over the years"

The doctor grinned. "Baby. Okay, that was the last one. You can pull your trousers up."

He peeled off his gloves and threw the used syringe into a special bin that his nurse held out for him.

"You may experience some flu-like symptoms over the next twenty-four hours, and you'll probably get some localized bruising, but if you feel any worse than that, give me a call. When are you traveling?"

"Ten days' time." Brock smiled and got to his feet. "Then I'll be out there for four weeks. I know I should have come in sooner."

"Yes, you should. Still, better now than not at all. Well, good luck. Stay safe. Bring me back another picture for the wall in reception."

Brock pulled the consulting room door closed behind him but still overheard the doctor as he said, "Colombia! I don't know whether he's brave, stupid or just too young to know any better!"

Brock waited for the nurse to respond, but nothing happened.

"Linda! Quit mooning over him and get the room ready for the next patient."

"But he's so gorgeous, Doc. I could definitely be tempted to get unprofessional with him!"

Brock winced. *Not in this lifetime.*

The doctor chuckled. "Forget it! He's more likely to go for me than you."

There was a groan. "Oh, for goodness sake, I know it's a cliché, but I'm going to say it anyway. Why are all the pretty ones either married or gay? That is a serious loss to womankind."

Brock shook his head, stepped away from the door then headed for the exit. He didn't mind the comments. Linda said the same thing every time she saw him, and, as he used his brother's house a lot when he was traveling, that was frequently. Outside the surgery, the weather was doing its best impression of a tropical monsoon, though without the heat. The rain beat down onto pavements already awash after days of continuous downpours. In the distance, thunder rumbled ominously and the sky had a threatening purple hue that spoke of more rain to come.

Brock looked up just as lightning split the sky. The rain got even harder. He turned up the collar of his waterproof coat and grimaced at the trickle of cold water that immediately slid down his neck. In seconds, his hair was soaked and plastered to his head. He hunched his shoulders and lengthened his stride toward home—though it wasn't strictly *his* home. He was just house-sitting while his brother, sister-in-law and two young nephews spent their annual fortnight's holiday on one of the Balearic Islands—he couldn't remember which one.

Brock spent such a lot of time traveling on photographic assignments that he'd never bothered to get his own place. When he was in England, he spent the time with his brother's family or returned to his mum and dad's rambling old place in Northumberland. Their house was so big, and they were both so busy with various pet projects and charities, that he could probably have lived there full-time without them even noticing his presence. Brock smiled to himself at the thought—he was very fond of his eccentric parents.

He soon arrived at the edge of the new estate where his brother's house sat on a decent-sized plot, halfway down a tree-lined avenue. Despite the miserable weather, he felt uncomfortably warm and was glad to make it to the sanctuary of the front hall, where a small puddle gathered around his feet as he stripped off dripping outdoor clothes and boots. Feeling progressively worse, he caught his reflection in the hall mirror and grimaced. His skin appeared clammy and his hands shook a little.

"Bloody vaccinations," he muttered. He climbed the stairs slowly, passing a number of his own framed photographs, and headed for the guest room bed. "Better just sleep it off." He grabbed a towel from the en suite, gave his hair a rub then stripped to his underwear. Drawing the curtains, he frowned at the sheets of driving rain. He could just make out the shape of a man sheltering under a tree opposite the house. "Blimey, he must be soaked." Despite his desire to get into his comfy bed to sleep away the after-effects of his inoculations as quickly as possible, Brock shrugged into his dressing gown then went back downstairs to the hallway to grab an umbrella. If the guy had to be outside, at least he could stay a little drier. By the time he went to the front door, the man was gone. Had he even been there, or was it a side-effect of the injections the doctor hadn't warned him about? He trudged back to the bedroom, finished pulling the curtains closed then took off his robe. He slid gratefully between cool sheets as his body reacted to the cocktail of drugs swimming through his system. Sleep came quickly and he drifted into dreams of distant jungles and the amazing pictures he would take.

* * * *

Outside, under the dripping tree, Kyle Dawson shifted uncomfortably. He had just been treated to a glimpse of the most tempting body he'd seen in some time and his cock had started dancing to its own tune despite the cold, damp conditions. He shook water droplets from the caped shoulders of his long, waxed coat and tilted the brim of his hat forward a bit further.

Kyle knew exactly where the subject of his observation had been that day, indeed for the last two weeks, though today was the first time he had gotten close to Brock's home.

He closed his eyes and recalled the details of the file he had been given. *Lysander Brock, known as Brock to his friends* – parents clearly had a thing for Shakespeare because his brother's name was Ferdinand. *Six feet tall, blond hair, blue eyes* – stunning blue eyes in Kyle's opinion – *one-hundred-eighty pounds* – all completely edible – *aged twenty-five. Permanent address listed at his parents' home in Northumberland. Professional photographer with work published in every travel and wildlife publication worth reading. Very well-traveled, with skills that included caving, climbing and hiking. Currently unattached. Two previous boyfriends known, neither particularly serious.*

Or deserving, Kyle thought grumpily.

He pictured the photo hidden in his inside pocket and licked his lips. He knew he should be maintaining a cold, clinical approach to the task ahead but, for Christ's sake, this guy was stunning and there was no harm in dreaming. After all, he'd been chosen for the job specifically because he was also gay. His bosses had thought he would blend in better if he needed to follow his quarry to gay pubs and clubs, though, in the end, that had not been necessary. Lysander Brock led a very quiet life when he wasn't working.

"You'd have no chance, you idiot," Kyle muttered under his breath, "even if you weren't about to ruin his day."

He looked around to make sure he was unobserved then crossed the road. The appalling weather worked in his favor, as very few people were out and about. Confident that there was no one around to witness his swift journey across the garden and, through the unlocked gate, he slipped down the path at the side of the house and into the back garden of the property. Tall hedges and mature trees shielded it from the neighboring houses, giving him all the time in the world to pick the lock on the door and slip into the kitchen.

Kyle found the back door key on a wall hook. He relocked the door, slid the additional bolt shut and tucked the key into his pocket. Taking his time, he removed his wet coat and hat and hung them over a chair. The layout of the house was stored in his head so he moved confidently to the front door to set the deadbolts. Secure in the knowledge that Brock would not be able to run, he crept up the stairs and peered around the door of the guest bedroom. Kyle had to bite down on his lip as he saw the young man in the bed, sound asleep. Brock had pushed the covers down to his hips, one arm was flung out to the side and his smooth, hairless chest rose and fell gently as he breathed. His face was a little flushed but, other than that, he seemed at peace. Kyle resisted the temptation to pull the covers down a little farther, backed away then crept downstairs to the kitchen. He took one of the chairs set around the kitchen table and turned it so that he could face the door to the hall then he settled down to wait.

About the Author

Lucinda lives in a small village in the English countryside, surrounded by rolling hills, cows and sheep. She started writing to fill time between jobs and is now firmly and unashamedly addicted.

She loves the English weather, especially the rain, and adores a thunderstorm. She loves good food, warm company and a crackling fire. She's fascinated by the psychology of relationships, especially between men, and her stories contain some subtle (and some not so subtle) leanings towards BDSM.

L.M. loves to hear from readers. You can find her contact information, website details and author profile page at http://www.pride-publishing.com.